Sti[illegible]p Street

A. Alwan

Translated by: Dr. Dia Karooni

Mira Publishing House cic - 2015

Mira Publishing House

53F Blackmoor Road
Leeds LS1617 5LZ
West Yorkshire
England
www.MiraPublishing.com

Sticky Trap Street
By A. Alwan
ISBN 978-1-908509-09-3

First published in Great Britain 2015 by Mira Publishing House

Cover painting: The Road to L'Hermitage in Snow by Camille Pissarro

Also by A. Alwan: The Sheikh's Detective. ISBN 978-1-908509-00-0

British Library Cataloguing in Publication Data. A catalogue record for this book is available from the British Library.

MiR

About Sticky Trap Street

Sticky Trap Street is a highly symbolic novelette-cum-novella. It is neatly constructed and brilliantly thought out. This work of art sets the tone and the direction of the storyline right from the outset. All is gravitated towards the centre of imaginary little town, built in the shape of a trap, on a site previously used as a make-believe airfield, to mislead and trap the Nazis fighter planes, reminiscent of a spider web that entraps flying insects.

Every human character is moving in that direction. In brief, it is a story of trapping and entrapment, unfolding to reveal the deceit, hypocrisy and corruption that result from having different characters in a setting, pre-arranged for them. Each one depicts their own deceit, oblivious to the fact that they are all victims caught up in a trap. While their predicaments differ, they all seem to be doomed in a war-like game where the hunter becomes both hunted and haunted. The harder one attempts to get out of this impasse, the more entangled up they become; exactly like a trapped insect desperate for a way out. Amidst all this scramble, the author's dark humour and sarcasm permeates down to many of the characters in order to help the reader process their sudden and at times erratic reactions and also their mysterious demise.

The Translator

Chapter 1

People were caught off guard by the relentless snow. Weather forecasters claimed Britain had never seen the like for a hundred years. With its captivating slopes, Three Hills Town was suddenly transformed into a white sheet.

From a vantage point above the town, school children, like grey dots, could be seen plodding their way to school, plucking their sinking feet from the knee-high downy snow, missing out on the coveted fun of throwing snowballs because of the ferocious blizzard.

Time seemed to race past but there was no sign of the long awaited bus- instead, the wind continued to lash the road with gusts of powdery snow, filling up the potholes and burying the tracks left behind by cars' tyres.

The icy wind made David feel stiff. His feet were now frozen cold. His trousers were soaking wet. His legs began shaking uncontrollably and his upper torso started shivering. Yet, the thought of going back home to collect his overcoat and umbrella meant that he would be doubly delayed for work.

He had never been late for work before, regardless of the circumstances and so he realised that he was in a terrible predicament.

Encouraged by a small group of passengers, bored with waiting, and now making their way up the climbing road ahead, he finally trudged up behind. He joined a long line of marchers trekking their way up their feet sinking in the snow, with David's shoes skidding leftwards and rightwards. He felt a sensation of dampness creeping to the top of his head.

The Midland's winter could be anything but merciful in January and February. This year the northern wind and snowfall had arrived earlier than expected in November.

Mothers had not yet begun escorting their children to the nurseries; instead they kept to their kitchens, listening to the radio. But the broadcast of the Met Office did not reach the students who now spread across the passages and the footpaths that led to their schools. They missed out on all the fun of an unexpected, precious day off. They were, instead, received by half of the usual number of staff who ordered them to warm themselves up in classrooms without teachers.

Laziness alone prevented David from going back home to fetch his coat.

None of the rest of the employees, including the chairman, knows the password that would enable them to access the town's log of expenditure. It was a highly classified secret that David alone was privy to.

He realised now, more than ever, and in this atrocious weather the heavy and absurd burden of his responsibility!

The employees huddled in the Town Hall's doorway, debating and expressing their opinions, as David stamped his feet, kicked the snow off his shoes and swept it off his shoulders and trousers.

'Get that crown off your head. It looks like Richard the Third's!' shouted an employee, laughing.

David brushed his hair with both hands and swept the snow from around his ears, like someone trying to rid himself of a pile of spiders scurrying around his head.

'The chairman's Jag has sunk under the snow outside his mansion!' shouted an employee from the end of the corridor, 'and his deputy's wife is placing cold compresses on her husband's forehead. He has a cold!'

Another bellowed from the group that had gathered at the doorway, with more glad tidings 'She says on the telephone that he's come down with a fever and will be off sick today.'

A third said, 'I bet he has her head clamped between his thighs while she plays the flute for him!'

The crowd burst into laughter. Meanwhile another snow-covered gathering of employees stepped forward. They were slowed down by the queue at the entrance and visibly vexed by the weather.

The employee who had spoken first added, 'Half the staff, you know, have so far failed to turn up.'

Another commented, with an edge of sarcasm, 'We may safely consider them missing.'

The previous employee added, 'How can we work in this situation, when both the chairman and his deputy are absent?'

'The schools are closed for today, and perhaps tomorrow if the weather does not' improve.'

'This doesn't include the council, does it?' asked another. 'We have to deal with citizens' affairs, you know!'

'Even without snow we used to operate perfectly with only half our staff,' quipped another, before adding, 'but will somebody tell me why those who live just round the corner are still late!'

'Customers won't be coming today, anyway,' suggested another.

'Just you wait. Phone calls will soon start coming.' someone else remarked.

Finally one supervisor announced, 'It's almost ten o'clock, lads. There's no point hanging around here without good reason. Let's get inside.'

As the men sluggishly left the doorway, David continued brushing the remaining snow off his clothes and his hair. His spring clothes were soaked and he was shivering slightly despite the heater at the entrance opposite the main road. The road itself was abandoned by vehicles and the usual passersby. The snow continued to fall unabated, reaching a depth of two feet.

A vision of his wife floated across his imagination, trudging through the snow to her hair-dressing salon, opening the doors and shutters, and turning on the heating while waiting for her first customer.

'Female customers are always on time for a hair-dressing appointment,' he said to himself, shivering with cold, 'even when the snow rises as high as ten feet.'

***

On the early morning of the second of November, Fiona, David's wife, sneaked out the house, walking quickly, stumbling in the frozen snow. She headed towards the bank on Sticky Trap Street. It was nestled between several shops and was quite unremarkable in appearance. She left her husband in deep slumber, mystified as to why he was so late going to the Town Hall.

She had patted his shoulder, but was not really keen to wake him. With difficulty he opened one eye then both, but it was as though his eyelids were stitched together. This was her chance to dash out. When she reached Sticky Trap Street, she found a long queue of men and women, extending and snaking down the road and getting round and round for about three hundred metres or thereabouts, finally stopping at the entrance of the bank. She halted, hesitant, but more people joined the line that was growing at an amazing rate. Fiona lined up behind a woman, stretching her sight further to the far end of the street. She asked 'Where does this line end?' 'At the bank as you can see!' said the woman. Fiona stood in line joining the throng. She noticed a calm and quintessentially English smile on their faces and thought that they were noticeably avoiding eye contact and also interaction with one another.

It was not a convenient time for banks to do business, as it was sometime before nine o'clock. Yet, the queue stretched far behind her. She felt uneasy about asking any more questions. Everyone was quiet and wearing a satisfied smile. She felt in her bag to ensure the cheque was still safely tucked inside. She waited, tense, for the clock to strike nine. Her mind was going through her bag and back to the queue where everyone seemed reticent about why they were visiting the bank at that particular hour. She would not feel comfortable until she reached the bank teller's window. She would then ask why there were so many customers lining up at such an early hour. She left the house a short time before David left for the Town Hall. She was aware that that day was not a bank holiday, a weekend, or any national holiday. It was not even preceded by an unexpected suspension of business declared by the government. So, what on earth was going on?

At 10 a.m. she finally reached the entrance of the bank and peered through the glass. The queue had branched now into five new queues, each moving in an orderly fashion towards a counter where bank employees were hard at work, like robots, filling handbags and wallets to capacity with bank notes. Some customers carelessly left their receipts behind, others simply ignored them. All was running smoothly and rapidly. Throughout the process the bank staff were being prompted by the manager, who was shifting around and, at times, even handing out wads of cash after the machines had run dry.

On entering, Fiona overheard the manager yelling into the telephone from his office. 'Send me cash as fast as you can! Make it double quick! Cash from the Central Bank, cash from the branches, cash from anywhere you can. Cash at any cost.'

When she stood in front of the cashier's window and presented the documents that confirmed her name and address, he returned them to her without even checking and gave her two huge wads of money which disappeared quickly into her bag. There were beads of sweat on his face. He scarcely had time for a smile or a welcoming gesture. She left, clutching her hand-bag against her heaving breasts. She was still shaking in disbelief. She walked directly to the hair-dressing salon. It was long past ten o'clock.

That evening, after Fiona returned from work, she squatted before David and asked, 'David, can we talk?'

'Yes. What's wrong?'

She faced his downcast eyes. 'Are you being threatened, David?'

'You've asked me this question several times before and I've answered you,' he grumbled, without lifting his eyes.

'I will still ask you until I know!' she replied resolutely. 'I'm your wife, for God's sake. I have to know. Tell me, David, is your life being threatened?'

'I don't think so,' he responded, with an air of nonchalance.

'Why did they have to drag you out of your sickbed? And why would an employee have to escort you right to the door of the house?'

Without facing her, he looked upwards and explained, 'The chairman says it was for my own safety. That's all I know.'

'That means your safety is at risk, David! Tell me! What have you done? I need to know!' She squatted on the floor, not letting him move, focusing her eyes on him from below.

'I did nothing, believe me.' He spoke sadly and

defensively.

'How come you do not do anything, and the whole world is fuming with rage around you?' She slapped both knees in exasperation.

A few days earlier David had been suddenly struck down by fever. He became prone to frequent bouts of absent-mindedness in which he lost his sense of awareness and became oblivious to everything around him. In the mornings he felt cold, despite being well wrapped up, and was now down with fever until a council car later turned up and he was dragged out of his bed.

As his wife squatted before him he smelt the salon's perfume that clung to his hands and to his wife's clothes. He had always loved this mixture, which set female hairdressers apart from other women. Something resembling affection kindled within him, floating through his imagination like a cloud. He remembered the days when he used to open the door to the salon to say hello on his way home. The female assistants would reply with the familiar, 'Hi David!' accompanied by smiles, blown through a warm whiff of perfume, permeating his senses and intoxicating him.

He wanted to console her and ease his own perturbed soul. He leaned forward, pulled her toward him, and kissed her on the forehead. 'I don't remember doing anything to warrant this treatment, but they claim I gave the computer a command to release thousands of cheques to the residents of Three Hills.'

Fiona jerked back, her eyes wide open in panic. Her hands hung momentarily, frozen by her side. Then she gradually regained her calm and gathered herself together.

'Did you do that, David?'

'That's what they say. But I don't remember, believe me.' came the answer.

'You didn't, but you do not remember?' she was confused 'Did you send out cheques to all the residents of Three Hills?'

'That's what my boss is saying,' he responded incredulously.

'What was the value of these cheques? If you can remember…' Her voice had dropped to a whisper as if she were interrogating him.

'Ten thousand pounds, so they claim.'

She stood up and began pacing up and down the living room, pondering over his admission, mulling it over and repeating it to herself. 'Ten thousand pounds. Therefore every one received the same amount.'

***

On the second of November, the council chairman

came to regard the whole issue as a dark secret to be buried deep inside his office along with the other secrets. However, it was like ember, burning slowly yet inexorably towards the core, setting fires inside his heart and sending smoke up to the roof of his bald head, depriving him of the delectation of sleep and the delight of prosperous family news. It spoiled his happiness when reading government appraisals of the town's achievements, and threatened the increase in the annual budget of the local authority. It also spoiled his enthusiasm for the profits from the companies contracted to carry out road maintenance and fill up potholes.

In short, the issue had threatened his happiness or, rather, his varied sources of happiness. The council chairman, Mr Hudson, had paid the missing amount out of his own personal account— a dark secret he shared only with his deputy. He quickly forced the employees in charge of printing out the cheques into early retirement and swore them into absolute silence, and subsequent journalists were barred access to the council.

He sent a fact-finding committee to the residents of Three Hills with the proviso that they made no mention of the cheque except surreptitiously in order to gain information.

Yet, the committee failed to discover any tangible fact since the Three Hills residents had kept absolutely quiet. Each resident carefully denied any knowledge of the cheque they had each received. A hush had fallen upon the town.

Mr Hudson was relentless. He created a small committee of computer experts and demanded that they pinpoint the defect, so as to distract their attention from the core of the conundrum.

He claimed that an amount of twenty pence had been sent out to every resident in Three Hills. How did that happen? Who caused it? And, how come the central system, which had never before issued or printed all the names and addresses in one go, received the command and executed the release of that amount to each and every address in Three Hills without exception?

On uttering his final word, Mr Liam Hudson hit the table with his fist, smoke streaming out of his ears, nostrils and mouth as he spoke. He then stormed from one room to another without any direction or purpose, and finally remained rigid, with his head, neck and palms running with sweat that seeped down to his feet.

When his secretary, Rose Bennet, saw smoke rising in long, thin bands, trailing behind him everywhere he went, she observed him for a while and she approached him at the earliest opportunity and said with a voice of guarded humility, 'Excuse me, Mr. Hudson, what's this smoke encircling your head?'

He snapped back through gritted teeth, 'Don't you see the biting, chilly weather?' Then in a voice hardly audible, he murmured under his breath, 'You cow.'

Rose was by no means a cow. Neither did she resemble one whether from a distance or on close inspection.

Her upper body was slender. The lower part provocatively plump. She was reasonably beautiful.

Rose would often remember how once she ran in high heels in a street full of frozen potholes, how she had slid and fallen on her rump, and at times on her face. Crying out behind a procession of journalists and senior staff members, who joined the chairman in his sport—which he had invented after a heavy fall of snow—jogging in a vest and a pair of shorts.

'Mr Hudson! Mr Hudson! The bank manager wants to talk to you regarding an urgent matter! Very critical, Mr Hudson!' She kept running after the chairman's athletic procession.

Liam was obviously braving the cold weather, setting himself up as an example to the rest of the citizens as a man who did not fear the freak weather, however bitter it might turn.

He turned back in response to her hoarse cries. She was holding a mobile phone high in her hand and panting as she approached, looking at his blood-circulated, ruddy legs, staring at them lustfully, trying to catch her spasmodic breath. She said, in words interrupted alternately by inhalation and exhalation, 'Forgive me, Mr Hudson. It's the bank manager… urgent call… very urgent!'

The council chairman smiled, begging his procession's indulgence for the interruption, which he thought unjustifiably urgent. After a quick apology to all those around him he reluctantly took the mobile phone. Mrs Bennet released the phone from her frozen grip and rested her eyes upon the area between Liam's thighs. Something stirred within her.

He said, 'Thank you, Mrs Bennet'; then, into the mobile phone, a broad smile radiating across his face, 'Hello… Thank you, Mr Rodi. I'm doing my workout. Ha ha… Wish you could join me too. Ha, ha, ha, yes! Say that again, please… How much did you spend?'

The smile was wiped off his face, with hesitation he asked again, 'How much did you spend? I'm sorry, you will have to repeat that… Did you say Three Hills? Ten… Oh my God. Stop issuing those bloody cheques immediately! You have already sent out all the cheques? All of them? Oh, God in heaven!'

***

On the third of November, the computer experts prepared a report, concluding that, 'While it is true that the system does not execute a command with a thousand addresses at one go, it may still respond to a command like that in exceptional circumstances. It could print the addresses on the envelopes and the cheques on separate papers to a thousand households. However, this is an extremely rare event, when the program retrieves and displays all the information about a specific area. This requires a number of commands to be carried out by someone. Never before has information flowed out on its own, particularly when printing on paper is called for!'

'So, it was David who gave the command?' enquired Mr Hudson, suppressing the noise produced by his teeth grinding together.

David was questioned for the twentieth time. It was the same question: 'why did you press the print key and how did the system respond in compliance with that command dragging along in one go a thousand addresses?'

Yet, David was consistent in stressing on every occasion his inability to remember.

He was provided with special care and protection within the council building. He was not to communicate with anyone. He was guarded by two employees who knew nothing about the command he had given to the system. Nor did they know about the cheques that were issued, and how they were distributed by the post office to the residents of Three Hills the following day.

Nothing about this event had been leaked to the

government at Downing Street. The council chairman had paid the amount in full from his private account. He paid ten million pounds to the bank, making sure the event was kept under wraps. As a result, Mr Hudson's bank balance had spiralled down by ten million in the course of just one day, without even gambling on the stock market, playing cards, buying a new building at auction at a very reduced price, or losing his hard earned wealth to a hacker!

David had indeed lost his power of recall, this was a fact that the council chairman, with a heavy heart had started to come to terms with. David could neither hear nor remember, with moments punctuated by bouts of unconsciousness. He would wonder away in a journey of delightful destructiveness, barring him from focusing on his mental powers. Had it not been for his memory decline, the interrogation sessions would have run into hundreds.

It was his wife who alerted the council to his condition. She conveniently found a pretext to make plans for their future since she had indeed received the cheque, taken it to the bank to receive the ten thousand pounds in her name, without telling him about It. She later hid the money in a parcel that she kept in a drawer in which she kept her underwear that were polluted by the perfumes of her profession; Vidal Sassoon, and the hair mordant.

The secretary could have been disadvantaged by

the council chairman's catastrophe, which seemed to have been overlooked – calamity rather which she was afflicted with- the adversity that spoiled his temperament. While she was the ever spoiled one, ranking first in his order of priorities, she had now sadly been downgraded and labelled as a 'cow', in his bouts of fury and annoyance with everyone around him, albeit in a low voice, this became louder to the point that he started calling her 'stupid' whenever she suggested that he should take it easy and that he ought to forget about his domestic problems—the nagging of his wife—by coming with her to the 'shrine', to sleep in her warm lap and bosom – But, she remained oblivious as to the real reason why smoke climbed out of his ears and nose in an ever-spinning vortex.

The small room they named the 'sanctum' was devoted to the chairman's siestas and the nightly 'conquests' that were the real reason for his delayed return home at night. It was adjacent to his spacious office. He shuffled into it through a door often kept locked—the rest of the employees were neither allowed to get through it nor find out about its sparse furniture which was carefully chosen; it contained cups, a coffee machine for making espresso coffee and a small fridge in the corner, which contained the finest types of whisky and brandy.

It was only the secretary who had possession of the

key to the 'sanctum'. She was the one who arranged phantom meetings for Liam. Meanwhile, the chairman's thighs, now ruddy and sweating from jogging, set Rose Bennet's sexual fantasies on fire for a few days.

***

The blizzard did not continue to batter the north of England and the Midlands as forecast by the radio and TV stations. However, the downpour continued to lash the streets of Three Hills, cleansing them from the snow.

The morning sunshine was moderate enough to thaw the snow, but it remained on the roads whose eastern edges had been left in the shade.

The people had found at last something to joke about in the stupidly predicted weather forecast.

It transpired that the global tilt of the orbit was but a pessimistic myth circulated by some scientist somewhere obsessed with global warming.

The children returned to school, playing happily. Mothers dropped their children at the nurseries and went back to their kitchens, content with the glorious weather.

People emerged with their various dogs—Rottweiler, shepherd, boxer—on their human hunt, hunting the English, relishing their fresh flesh.

Civil servants left hurriedly in their cars on route to

their departments and offices.

Fiona had woken early that morning, shaking and staring in disbelief, on the way to the bank in Three Hills. She had to collect the money before the government detected the blunder. If there had been an error, that is. Thousands of comments have been made in the newspapers and a similar number of racy jokes have been also made about the radio announcers. A most widely read and a more balanced newspaper suggested that a trillion tons of cement was made available to build a dam, three kilometres wide and fifty kilometres high all along the north west of the South Pole until the globe had recovered its natural curve along the axis.

She spent the rest of her day in the salon, exchanging banter with the customers, spoiling them with great amounts of shampoo and hair spray. But her mind was elsewhere. She found her thoughts drifting to the drawer at the back of the salon, in which the handbag containing the money had been placed under lock and key.

When the clock struck four, the council security guards had arrived. One of them asked, 'Are you David's wife?'

'Yes,' she replied.

'Where could he be now, please?' he calmly asked, showing a great deal of respect.

'In the council building, I suppose', she replied in

mock astonishment, her mind still in the drawer where the money was hiding.

'No, he has not turned up today at the council building. Where do you think he might be?'

She was confused and hesitant as though she was being accused. 'I assumed, as I said, that he had gone to the council building!'

She was overtaken with fear but quickly regained her composure. 'When I left he was asleep with fever. I was certain he would go soon after he woke up.'

'Would you mind accompanying us to the house, just to make sure?'

'Certainly…' she responded, disconcerted.

She went to the back of the salon to tell one of the assistants to continue looking after the business. She then unlocked the drawer, took out her handbag, pressing it as hard as she could against her chest, and led the two guards toward the house.

On entering the house, she was surprised to find her husband deep in his slumber, as she had left him in the morning.

The two guards lifted him and shoved him into a car parked outside the door and sped off toward the council building, while David was still half asleep.

Until six, all the chairman's attempts to find out what prompted David to give the command to the computer, and why the system complied with the printing and releasing of payments, were to no avail.

David continued to open and close his eyes, repeating the mantra, 'I don't remember.'

Fiona realised that all Three Hills residents had received ten thousand pounds on the morning of the first of November, without exception. They did not communicate with each other about it. Moreover, she learnt that it was David who committed that error while he was fiddling with the computer. She hid the money for herself without telling him. She pretended to be concerned about his partial deafness and absent-mindedness, which had become a daily occurrence, and she did not talk to him about the subject except evasively or remotely, asking how his day had been. She did not talk to him about the data stored up on the council's servers neither did she talk to him about how this data was classified into towns and villages in their relevant provinces, so much so that the command to pay out the cheques to Three Hills was genuine but suspended when the rest of the cities was involved!

She went to great lengths to keep her husband calm and alone, away from prying eyes. Once his fever had relaxed its grasp, she might ask him, for instance, about the nature of his computer work. Then she would ask an innocuous question. 'Has it ever happened before that all data about the county, its cities and villages, has been retrieved with one single command?'

Distractedly, he would say, 'No.'

'Why?' she prompted him, exploiting his moment of consciousness.

'We work in accordance with a system that is supposed to gather information and classify it. The information is often channelled across a number of applications which are, in turn, distributed into numerous servers.'

'Very well, but can the government access your work?'

'The government uses another incompatible system. I mean, it can't.' he said, showing signs of stress as though he had overstrained himself as he had shed all that he could remember as regards his knowledge of the programs of the system.

Fiona said afterward, 'Thank you, darling. You may go back to your absent-mindedness, which calms your nerves.'

She was convinced the money would remain safe, since the government could not force people into returning all or any of it. And as long as David did not fully understand the situation, the money would ultimately be hers alone.

Fiona kept that information to herself. She had never uttered a single word about it to the neighbours. Nor did she find the neighbours willing to talk about the subject either.

The customers who came to the salon often talked about everything but the cheques, which they had received and cashed on the same day. Their replies to her ambiguous questions were in the form of broad smiles.

Fiona had a personal computer which she used in dealing with her customers. She was able to log on and off with ease. She watched online the up-to-date haircuts, fashionable clothes and everything that dealt with women's affairs, whims and desires. However, she did not know anything about the programs that ran it and from her latest talk with David, who was now half-deaf and quite oblivious to what was going on around him, she learnt that each system of such programs belonged to a certain software company that had sole monopoly which allowed it to have full control of its marketing to industries, big organisations and state departments.

Each system was different from the other. The government had its own unique operating system which was different, praise the Lord, from all those operated by the town councils. All those computer systems belonged to multiple and different companies and that the marketing of these IT applications is a global business, and hence, unstable. Despite the prevalence of potential informers across the town, all attempts to tease out one confession from a single person who had received the ten thousand pounds failed. The Three Hills residents remained resolutely silent despite the fact that the bills of the payment bore their signatures. The bank was forced to be discreet about this and kept it concealed from the government.

They were bitter, depressing and sad days beset with fury and teeth grinding as far as Mr. Hudson was concerned, aggravated by the rage and wriggling caused by the suppression of the secret for as long and keeping it under lock and key so that it might not leak into Downing Street.

It now appears that Mr. Hudson's attempts to find a legal gap that would allow him to retrieve the ten million pounds from Three Hills residents, through any sort of settlement, had failed miserably. No one in town would confirm receipt of the money lest they should be forced to return it. Should Mr Hudson resort to force, given that signatures appeared on the bills of payment, someone might challenge that by alerting the central government and in so doing, the days ahead would then become more intolerable and that would surely end in real disaster that would attract a probe into the sources of his wealth!

As an experiment it occurred to the disturbed council chairman to instruct the computer department to send a letter to five hundred residents in Three Hills with a cheque for twenty pence each to be paid to the households as a rule to secure admission of receipt that would ensure the retrieval of the earlier amount. It would then be a test case that rested on the fact that it was an unintentional computer error which might happen at any department that had led to the blunder.

But on the following day, all the cheques and the standard letters were returned to the council with a note stating, 'Our dear council does not owe us the amount of twenty pence; therefore, we hereby return the cheque and the attached letter.'

Mr Hudson hit his forehead with his hand with force, staring askance at the returned cheques and letters. The secretary stood watching with sorrow that is laden with lust, the perplexity of the chairman which she has not been able to find a feasible reason for a reason that has kept the shrine locked for ten critical and unbearable days. This despite the fact that she kept removing another piece of clothing to the extent of going naked before his eyes, which were sometimes wide open, staring blankly, and at other times closed tightly, hiding some unfathomable sadness.

The secretary was suppressing a burning lust that had not yet subsided since the second of November, when she glimpsed the council chairman's dewy, moist and manly thighs. However, when her husband's hand surreptitiously slid over her ample rump it prompted words of reproach. 'You want to push the piston into the cylinder every day, don't you, without getting satiated?'

He abruptly withdrew his hand, surprised she should mention the phrase 'every day' for she had never responded favourably to his advances for three months. Tonight, he was thinking of making love to her to ease her insomnia and alleviate the torture of her turning over again and again in the bed.

She blamed herself for not appreciating the provocation of the two thighs, when they were dripping with sweat, turning red like roses, almost bursting with blood.

She visualised herself kneeling before him, hugging the thigh, kissing it and, like a hungry bee, sucking on its nectar, moving upwards, sensing the collision of her forehead with the hard thing, before moving up against it. She closed her eyes for fear of being found out by those standing next to her, then opened them with a long, whooping sigh of deprivation.

It was then that an urgent demand by Mr Hudson brought her back to planet Earth.

'Bring David over from the office and make sure he is awake!'

David was duly dragged into the chairman's office. They were waiting for his bouts of wakefulness and the recovery of his hearing. Only on this occasion the chairman did not ask if David was fit and well enough to be questioned.

Chapter 2

In the winter of 2020, on the first of November, David suffered early senile dementia and a partial loss of hearing. The council announced the date in the big, unsteady script of Mr Liam Hudson, the council chairman, across a white sheet of paper half a metre in width. It was hanging above the side of his table, showing two dates: A catastrophic one that had to be remembered by all staff, with their accounts and reports evaluated against it; and the second which showed flexibility, clarity, and signs of efficiency, stability and lauded achievements.

David was referred to a large number of medical specialists, psychologists, otolaryngologists, and memory experts, and he was subjected to modern radiology. He was twice sent to the Capital to have his condition studied. There, he was laid naked in full view of a crowd of specialists who were allowed to turn him about, over, upright and upside down, probe and scrutinize every part of his body; testing his nerves, monitoring his blood circulation, arteries; and in the end sending him back to Three Hills with the professional opinion that 'he is physically sound, yet likely to be stricken with early dementia and partial deafness.'

David's hard-to-diagnose condition was left to time, as time alone could only ensure the decoding of the insolvable enigmas. Only time could tell. He would either regain his full consciousness and sense of hearing or spend the rest of his days keeping awake for a short while, then slipping back into a lapse of memory. The tests were conducted in absolute secrecy under the council chairman's supervision. The principal reason had been withheld from others, and the whole issue was hushed up. A completely binding silence was imposed on all employees around him and those who had printed the cheques, put them in envelopes and mailed them. At the beginning, minders were assigned to escort him home on the pretext of providing him with protection. However, when the council chairman became certain that the residents of the small town of Three Hills did not wish to break their silence on the subject—rather, they seemed to ruminate over the secret in their stomach—the alleged protection came to a halt. Liam Hudson remained staring with grief at that date, jotted in his own shaky hand. He hit his forehead with his clenched fist and let out a cry. 'How did all this happen?'

No one knew the reality of what had happened to David. Still, the eyes of the council chairman and his deputy, who were questioning him, were fixed upon him. He found himself unable to respond. He put his hands around his head in a tight clasp but was still unable to remember. Bits and pieces from the morning of the first of November visited him, only for him to be overwhelmed by a sense of loss, hurled back into oblivion. He remained powerless, unable to talk; unable to comprehend why he was there, being interrogated.

David was dragged into the council chairman's office. He was seated, surrounded by piles of envelopes returned by the post office, along with the ten-pence cheques. And although they would normally wait for him to regain his awareness and become fully alert, the council chairman on this occasion however, did not bother to ask whether or not he was fit to be questioned.

Mr Hudson asked the officials who brought the letters to leave the room. The deputy, however, was allowed to stay. Meanwhile the secretary, who was wholly lost in her fantasyland, was told to close the door and go back to her room.

When the three were on their own, the council chairman took his deputy aside, away from David's hearing which, in itself, served no purpose,

'These letters will be relied on in court and will be used against us; and despite the randomly selected addresses, the residents of the accursed Three Hills have returned the cheques, which confirms they have not mishandled any money sent to them. What are we going to do now?'

He turned towards David, his face wilted through many a sleepless night, weighed down by worries. The areas surrounding his eyes were black. Smoke rose from his head in waves. He examined his quarry before finally pouncing.

The deputy, John Pickard replied, 'Mr Hudson, the use of the phrase "against us" is unhelpful. I would rather you used the phrase—'

'What?' the council chairman furiously cut in.

'I would rather you said "my interest and your interest", if you don't mind!' the deputy mumbled incoherently.

'I have heard the like of this so many times before!' He was enraged, steam rising from his head. 'And now that you are adding "my interest" and "your interest", do you see who has incurred more losses than the other? Are these your own words or were they suggested by that honourable wife of yours?'

'Believe me, Mr Chairman, the family has nothing to do with it. I am only acting out of concern. I only wanted you to point out which of the two aggrieved parties was hit harder in this very case.'

Trying to control the impulse to yell at Mr Pickard, Mr Hudson raised his fist higher and opened it in the air turning to the brightly lit ceiling for help against the resourcefulness of his naive and stupid deputy. Then he added through clenched teeth, that had taken a heavy toll through grinding, 'With regard to Mr.

Pickard's program and because of David, I have already paid ten million pounds out of my own account, lest his mistakes should attract the attention of 10 Downing Street!'

Mr. Pickard held his breath, wiped the beads of perspiration from his face and double chin, then opened his round eyes that resembled those of a chameleon. He said in astonishment, 'Was the error inherent in the OPCAL program we are currently using, Mr Hudson?'

'What have I been saying for the last ten wretched days, in which you spent your time sleeping like a baby?'

'I beg your pardon, Mr Hudson. I was ill in fact, lying in bed as the cold compresses and my poor wife would testify!'

Now the council chairman yelled at the top of his voice, 'Oh Heck! Spare us the testimony of your wife's compresses! It was OPCAL that brought us all these problems, Mr Pickard, through this idiot sitting here!' He pointed at David who sat on a chair, hardly hearing and scarcely perturbed by the shouts of the council chairman that ripped through the heart of everyone.

Eventually, Mr Hudson suppressed the fury boiling inside him. 'Firstly, I'm looking for a way to claw back my money from the residents of Three Hills. The amount of ten million pounds! Every time I think about it I die with rage and blaze once again. Secondly, this twerp sitting opposite gave the command to release those cheques. Thirdly, we pay the accursed OPCAL, every two or three months, two hundred thousand pounds in the name of maintenance, but the system does not operate properly and you are responsible on that account. Have I made myself clear, Mr Pickard?'

Mr. Pickard responded after some time, still wiping sweat from his face. 'If the situation is as you describe it, Mr Hudson, I will contact OPCAL now and ask them to carry out further maintenance!'

As he picked up the receiver to make the call the council chairman wrested the telephone from his grip, putting it back on its cradle. 'Are you an absolute idiot? I said we need to verify David's story first! Think of something else, Mr Pickard, for hell's sake!'

'If you say so.' The deputy was, totally baffled and confused. 'Yes, we need to think of something else, Mr Hudson!'

Two sharp taps on the door seized their attention. It opened slowly to reveal the secretary

'Have you called me on the phone, Mr Hudson?'

'Go back to your room, Mrs Bennet. No one called you.' He added, after she had withdrawn, closing the door behind her, 'I have been afflicted with dumb beasts of burden!'

The use of the word 'beast' was deliberate and appropriate in reference to the deputy chairman. Mr Pickard, a stumpy figure, was usually absent many days of the year. For various reasons, the council chairman had invariably wanted him to be simultaneously absent and present. He could take important decisions, unopposed, in his absence. However, when he was present he could be assigned minor tasks.

The deputy often came to his office with a handkerchief in his hand, never parting with it, wiping sweat from his face and his droopy double chin, in summer and winter alike. Wet and sweat-drenched handkerchiefs were always replaced by fresh ones, from his right pocket, and the wet ones placed in his left pocket.

The chairman had deliberately chosen his deputy from among his pathetically hopeless employees, so they say. He tended to be laid back and lazy by nature. He had relatively long service to his name. At times, he was called upon to attend the inauguration of minor council projects; but he was deliberately kept at a distance, or relegated to the back seats, when huge projects were inaugurated and attended by a large number of journalists.

Whenever the tall young chairman, with the bright, infectious smile and the physique of an athlete, cut the ribbon at the inauguration of big projects, he overshadowed Mr Pickard, whose presence was hardly felt by any of the attendees. For these reasons, Mr Hudson had allocated him a slim cut of the gains from the council's porous financial system, which he could revel in with Mrs Pickard, who was accustomed to preparing hot and cold compresses to agree with her husband's climate-sensitive forehead.

David sat, shifting his eyes between the chairman and his deputy while they were engaged in discussion. He waited, knowing in advance the question that would soon be levelled at him and the words he had to respond with: 'I don't recall.' Then he would be dragged back into the tightly secured office, guarded by an employee, to ensure he did not come into contact with other employees.

'David,' the deputy asked through his perspiration, 'did you find it hard to activate OPCAL?'

'I don't remember,' said David.

The deputy inquired expectantly, 'Has OPCAL crashed?'

David only looked at the pile of letters and repeated, 'I don't remember.'

'Well!' the deputy now addressing the chairman, 'let's contact OPCAL and they can resolve the issue!' He trotted to the telephone.

The chairman was quick to stand in his way to prevent him from reaching the phone'Not now, Mr Pickard, not now! The crash might have occurred in the mind of this crazed man!' He pointed again at David.

'Yes, we need to understand why his memory has

crashed' and with this pronouncement he quickly dismissed the thought of making a call.

'David,' said the council chairman, assuming an air of equanimity, 'you are a highly committed employee and you have never taken a day off. It's all in your employment record. For that reason, we have fully trusted you and have entrusted you with the council data from A to Z. That means all the confidential documents and data of the council, starting with salaries and expenditure, through to communications, employees' addresses in all the towns and villages and every major or minor information item that is relevant to their lives and affairs. We have entrusted you with it all.' He took a breath. 'Now tell me, David', continued the council chairman, 'why did you instruct the program to issue cheques to the Three Hills households? Just answer the question. Think.'

David lowered his head, thinking, leaving the chairman and his deputy each in their agonised state. Then he lifted his innocuous, dreamy eyes and said, 'You've got to believe me, I don't remember doing that.'

The chairman tried hard to contain his anger. 'Then what is your memory of the first of November, when you sat before your computer, David? Did you, unaware, give that command negligently? Did all the addresses appear on the screen and then you unintentionally authorised the release of ten thousand pounds outto each and every household in Three Hills without exception?'

Having failed to elicit any response his fury swelled. 'Or was it the OPCAL program that automatically commanded and chose Three Hills over other towns and started typing the cheques and addresses, which flowed out to the printer, unhindered, without your meddling?'

After pressing his head, thinking and rethinking yet again, David sighed. 'I do not remember. I don't remember anything that happened that day.'

'Do you recall someone taking advantage of your forgetfulness to meddle with your computer? Please, David, try to remember!' The council chairman pleaded with him, exasperated, puffing up steam that encircled his head like a halo.

'I was slumped over the computer with my fingers still on the keys when they came in to wake me. I exited the program and shut down the computer. That's all I can remember, sir. I don't even know how I got home.'

'But your wife cashed the cheque on the following day. Her signature is on this document!' He lifted a file from his desk and shook it in David's face, giving him a challenging look. 'You want me to believe she didn't talk to you about the money? Can you explain that?'

'I don't remember. Nor do I remember her telling me about the money. If you want me to ring her up now to ask her about it, I will do that!' asserted David.

'No, not by phone! You're not allowed to discuss this subject on the phone. Do you understand?'

'I do, sir,' replied David in compliance.

The chairman continued to labour his point. 'All telephones in England are monitored!'

David began to retrieve part of his confused awareness and emerged gradually from his trance. His eyes darted between the council chairman and his deputy, as though asking for forgiveness for causing them any harm; or perhaps seeking an end to their questioning, which seemed to serve no purpose and which had turned him into a victim, like themselves.

The chairman continued scurrying around the office, thinking, with interlocking waves of smoke circling the room, tracing his restless movements and remaining above his head that was the epicentre of the catastrophe. He was thinking of the ten million he had paid, and wishing the council building was burnt down and in ruins. He would not then feel the heat smouldering in his guts, destroying his life, rendering it into a pitch-dark tunnel with no glimmer of light at the other end.

'Listen, David!' Suddenly the chairman had a bright idea that filled up his disturbed, smoke-filled head and ignited his inside. He felt as though he had been struck by an electric shock. He took off his jacket, rolled up his sleeves, then bent down over David and said with feigned cordiality, 'How much is your salary at the council now?'

'Seven hundred pounds a month, as far as I can remember,' replied David.

'Only seven hundred pounds? Damn it!' he exclaimed incredulously. 'All our secrets are safeguarded by an employee who receives seven hundred pounds a month! That's unfair! Not fair at all!' said the chairman, glancing at his deputy, who immediately nodded, confirming his belief that David's salary was indeed too low.

Then the chairman's eyes rested firmly on David. 'We shall increase your salary by fifty pounds a month as from this month. What do you think of the raise which, I am confident, will restore fairness here at the council?'

'I don't know, Mr Chairman, sir!' David met the chairman's direct gaze.

Prompt, enthusiastic approval came from the deputy, who cut in, 'We shall put fairness back on course, for the first time in the history of the council.'

The chairman irritated by his deputy's untimely interruption. 'I must still count on you to return the generosity of the council by working your special magic on your wife, to extract an official admission of receiving the ten thousand pounds.'

After some thinking, David promised, 'I will... If I remember, that is.'

'You will, David! That's a good boy!' Having said that he took a five-pound note from his pocket and gave it to David. 'This will make you remember!'

David took the fiver, oblivious of the drift of the gesture.

'Buy her some fine wine. Look after her... well, you know...' The chairman acted out some romantic moves. 'Say sweet words to her. Chat her up at the table. Let it be a night to remember! Tell her how appreciated your services to the council are, and about the salary increase which will open new horizons for you both. Show her some affection and court her as you would have done on the first night of your wedding. And then... And then... gradually a word of love here and a flirtation there... Try to draw her out and ask her about the money. Have you understood?'

'That is what my poor wife does to me in bed' whispered Mr Pickard to himself.

David, who was still holding the five pound note, had forgotten what it was doing in his hand. 'I will, Mr Chairman. But why have you given me this fiver?'

'It's for the magic supper. It's a gift from me to you to buy a bottle of wine with. Hold it tight. Don't you lose it, and don't forget your mission tonight. Do it for the good of the whole community.' Then he pressed the button that linked him to the secretary. The door opened and the secretary, overwhelmed by excitement, said, 'Did you call me, Mr Hudson?'

'Yes. Will you please take David back to his office and make sure other employees do not cluster around him.'

'Done, Mr Hudson. Anything else I can do for you?'

'Later. Now back to your grave for the time being.'

She led David by the hand and was about to leave when the chairman pulled her aside and whispered in her ear, 'Lest I should forget, write down: One hundred pounds to be paid out to David, under the subject: other expenditure.'

'By all means, Mr Hudson.' She left, unable to take her eyes off Mr Hudson until the door was closed.

Chapter 3

Cities are built at the whim of one individual or to satisfy a group's need to be near a river water source. Communities then grow gradually and their needs diversify to cover both banks of the river. Sumer was built on the Tigris, Cairo on the Nile, Great Rome on the Tiber, Paris on the Seine, London on the Thames and Beijing on the Yellow River, Yangtze. Three Hills, however, was built on the whim of a bank employee whose eventual motive was to take over the position of bank manager. Away from rivers, rivulets and creeks, the town sucked its water through a massive pipe from the Midlands. Water was carried via narrow pipes into its houses, which were built at random, spreading out from an airfield originally built to house some bogus, skeletal warplanes, made of carton and plywood, as a decoy, a trap, to bring down Nazi warplanes in World War II.

When the sun rises on the steppes of Three Hills, the upper town turns into a dazzling green, decorated carpet. The interwoven stonewalls that surround the pasture resemble a delicate cobweb encircling the town. A scatter of cattle herds and flocks of sheep gives Three Hills a romantic charm. The town ends with a mass of tightly packed houses, separated by narrow lanes. A single, straight, wide street, extending half a mile, runs through its centre. This is Sticky Trap Street, named after the airfield.

Just like other cities and towns, Three Hills has its share in the British Encyclopaedia, presenting its history and the geographical location for the tourists or hikers who follow the maps towards legendary places.

During the World War II, two farmers and their families lived in the valley, but the government secretly evicted the families temporarily. An airfield was hastily built near the huts in the middle of the valley. And a number of skeletal warplanes, made of cartons and timber, became daily targets for the Nazis' Semt, Stukas and Heinkels, launched from bases in Norway. At night, the British reposition the skeletal warplanes to hunt down the Nazis' launchers, which cannot find enough space to manoeuvre between the hills.

When the war was over the carton and plywood were collected and deposited in a British army scrap yard in the Midlands. The two farmers returned to their huts that were levelled to the ground during the war. They were paid a modest compensation, which allowed them to resume their monotonous lives raising cattle.

Things were not yet over at this point. During the 50s of the last century, the manager of one of the bank branches stood on top of one of the three hills and scanned the valley below. 'Who owns this pit?' he asked.

The escort who accompanied him on his leisure trips replied, 'The State.'

The manager hit on a smart project that whetted his appetite.

He said, 'Let everyone own a house.'

He paid the sum of fifty pounds to the State, and had the land registered as a non-profit, charitable trust, benefiting whoever was willing to purchase a plot of land on which to build a house.

The slogan sounded very enticing. Residents from nearby cities and the neighbouring countryside raced one another to buy and build. Bank branches became more responsive. Insurance companies were established with the support and guidance of the bank. Suddenly, building material offices started to emerge. Offices for design and consultation followed.

Three Hills, the name later given to the pit, witnessed thriving construction activity. In the process, the bank was biting off profits and interest on every single transaction. Business flourished. The branch manager was promoted to the position of manager at Capital Bank Headquarters. The slogan, 'Let everyone own a house', took off all over England.

Ten years later, many owners defaulted on their loans, and the bank moved to another activity, namely repossessing houses. These would be re-sold at higher prices due to the growth of the market. The bank, therefore, would harvest more profits and open newer branches to facilitate the process of clawing back still more profit, speeding up both the relinquishing and transfer of ownership.

The houses in Three Hills, ever lacking in modern design, piled up, expanding from Sticky Trap Street to the tops of the three hills. They were, nevertheless, a good model for banking and economics in general.

Be a house owner and we will suck your nectar drop by drop, then we cast you aside. We will offer you the joy of owning a house for a few days, after which you will spend the rest of your life under psychological pressure, ending in depression that resembles African malaria. Once you catch it, it will render you bedridden, abandoned, groaning alone, visited by only one person who will administer the same dose, not hoping to cure you but only to leave you in limbo, between life and death, until your final gasp.

Since that time the banks began to take control of the English economy, after industries and innovations were the dominant players.

At present, Three Hills' share of the austerity plan, set up by the council chairman and signed by his deputy, albeit without consulting him, swept over the town like a tsunami that battered the Pacific coasts, hitting services like transportation of the elderly to hospitals or caring for them at home; disrupting the weekly rubbish collection, maintenance of roads, sewage pipes services and provision of drinking water.

The number of postmen was cut back; electric power was periodically shut down. Nominal fees were levied on primary schools. Teachers deemed surplus were made redundant.

Two weeks later, all services were disrupted and Three Hills residents woke to find their drinking water disconnected. Electricity was rationed. After twenty days, sewage water overflowed into the streets and houses.

It was barely a month since the potholes were filled with asphalt, yet the roads were littered with poorly made surfaces, making driving dangerous on Sticky Trap Street. Stray cats had ripped rubbish liners and plundered their contents, which now exuded a stench.

Despite all that, bills continued to drop on the mats. People were quick to pick up the phone to make a complaint, only to be answered by an automated answering machine:

'Hold the line. Your call is held in a queue. Your call will be answered shortly!'

Then the caller's ear was filled with Strauss's deafening marching tunes. The caller would have to hang up after a long, tense wait, cursing the day that brought him down to Three Hills to settle.

-2-

In an untidy kitchen littered with bottles, small trivial artefacts, David sat at an old table looking at an unopened wine bottle, reminiscing about the many statements uttered in the council chairman's office. He was unable to recall all of them. Then he focused on the one pressing question that kept bothering him, which he wanted to ask his wife about. It was the cheque she had received. The rest of what was said—the shouting and the raging argument, the pleading for the benefit of everyone—were flying around, like a spray of fragments, in the void of his vacuous memory.

This morning, the investigative sessions did not include a repetitive format like "why, did you authorize it", which put exhausting pressure on his nerves. After such sessions he would leave the room, worn out, leaning against the official who guided him back to his office. At times the yelling and cries of the council chairman would suddenly transform into calm words which lapsed into pleading. 'For the public good, David!'

Yet, he could neither remember what was said nor understand what was exactly meant. It sounded to him like an uproarious, crowded pub at the weekend.

While he was waiting for his wife's return, he had a feeling, almost a conviction, that he had been to a meeting with close friends brought together by a misfortune, kept apart by their jobs. Then, each went their own way, hoping to meet again shortly. However, he wondered why there was a wine bottle on the food table in front of him.

When Fiona arrived an hour later, entering the kitchen, she was muttering, 'I always give the elderly ladies early appointments. Today they brought into my salon Mrs Waldmere at the last moment. She slept while her head was still in the super hair dryer. It took us a quarter of an hour to wake her up!'

She moved about the kitchen, sorting out her shopping between the refrigerator and the dining table, talking about her old customer who was fast asleep, placing what was for supper on the table, fetching the needed plates without seriously acknowledging David's presence. When he lifted his head, she said, 'Hi, David, how are you feeling today?'

However, she went on to set the plates and put the food on them. Then the wine bottle caught her attention. She lifted it and read its label. 'Who bought this cheap wine? Was it you, David?'

'Yes', replied David heedlessly, following her with two eyes over his shoulders, weighed down by too much thinking about the day's events.

'Wow! How did you remember?' She smiled. 'You seem to be getting better. But why did you select this cheap wine?'

'It was the council chairman who gave me five

pounds and asked me to buy some wine for supper,' David replied automatically.

Fiona returned the bottle to the table and squatted in front of him. She wanted to know the reason behind the council chairman's unanticipated gesture.

'Why? What's behind this overly generous act, David?' she asked, concerned how he would react.

He was bending a little, trying to bring his thoughts into focus. Then he answered, 'So that you can tell me about the cheque which you received from the council.'

She jumped like a stung woman. 'What cheque is the council chairman talking about? I have not received any cheque in your name or in mine!'

David replied with naivety not compatible with the situation, Fiona understood. Yet she did not want to admit it, 'A cheque for ten thousand pounds.'

'I did not receive this amount, David!' Fiona replied resolutely.

She sat on the chair, edging closer to David, hugging him. 'I swear I do not understand anything of what the council chairman is saying!'

Fiona No doubt, had been through quite a lot in life since childhood. Her presence in the market taught her how to deal with different people, and how to handle each secret and keep it closely guarded and dear to her heart. She took encouragement from the realization that the satisfied Three Hills residents, having received this huge amount effortlessly, like her, were keeping it secret. They never talked about it. They did, however, believe that it was manna from heaven, a source of happiness. Each would feel it, to make sure it was there, to reassure themselves of their future—a reassurance that almost eluded them. They had always pinned their hopes on the state for attention and compassion.

'Come over here, darling, let's have supper; and while we have here this worthless wine, let's drink a little of it with the meat slices I have brought you.'

She opened the bottle of wine, then rose to fetch two elegant crystal glasses and then asked, 'Do you remember this set of glasses we got for the wedding present?' She examined the two glasses, eyeing them admiringly. Then she said, 'It was Mum's present! We haven't used them for ages!' She poured some wine then lifted her own glass. 'Let's celebrate the recovery of your memory back to its former glory! Chin! Chin!'

David lifted his glass, meeting hers nonchalantly. 'Chin! Chin.'

She pressed a piece of meat into his mouth. 'Eat it, my love. It will strengthen your memory, too.'

After chewing up the slice he said, 'But did you receive a cheque from the council?'

'Oh! David! I swear to you, no! Are we going to spend the night talking about the council chairman's delusions? Just drop the subject; or forget it, which is even better. Let's drink and have supper without the "council". Have you tried this cheese? It's French. Open your mouth!' She lifted a piece of cheese and pushed it into his mouth. 'Try it. The taste will linger for a while. God, it's hot in here.' She slightly pulled her shirt and said: 'Help me take off this shirt, please.'

Her chest appeared with all its charm, after David had carelessly removed her shirt. Fiona had an ample bosom, supported by an under-sized bra, and tender-skinned arms. She was of a medium height and reasonably plump and of a medium height, any playing of the coquette usually stimulates the imagination of the husband and put him in the mood for fun in bed.

Fiona placed one pretty pink arm around David, behind his back and with the other she lifted the food to his mouth. Or she would raise it at times, involuntarily, instinctively, as if to ward off the heat, but actually to give out the intoxicating heat of femininity, an explosive mixture of sweat, salon perfume and keen sexual urge.

'I didn't tell you about how Mrs Waldmere fell asleep under the super-hood drier, did I? Oh! She came in leaning against her carer, late for the appointment. After we washed her thin hair that resembled a muddled bunch of lily seedlings, we put the super-hood dryer machine over her wet hair. Her head sank in it and we could no longer see her. It appeared that the hood's warmth had claimed her. Meanwhile, her carer was leafing through the magazines, completely forgetting about Mrs Waldmere. We were busy tidying up the saloon, getting ready for closing time, you know. The assistant, Lisa was chatting away, putting the tools back where they belonged. Suddenly she remembered my customer. Only when she saw her carer engrossed in reading did she realise the seriousness of her oversight. She lifted the hood-dryer and whispered, "Mrs Waldmere! Mrs Waldmere!" She was fast asleep! Ha, ha, ha, my God! Mrs Waldmere didn't want to wake up! Honestly, I thought she had died in the chair.

Fiona carried on with her story:' "Psst psst!" I said to Lisa. "She's like a little kitten. Say 'psst' to her." And she quickly woke up. Oh my God!'

David, who was now eating slowly or, rather, taking the morsels from Fiona's hand, remained quiet. The tale seemingly had no effect on him. Fiona poured some more wine.

'It's true,' she said, 'it's cheap but at least it stirs up heat in the body. Drink up, my love! Relax! It's been a hard day's work from the beginning till the end. The second assistant was two hours late, making up excuses. I said to her, "Suzi, I do accept your apology, so why do you have to repeat yourself all day long?" I said to her, "I work here, too, like yourself. What if the saloon proprietor suddenly walks in and sees the saloon so piled up with waiting customers? Put yourself in my shoes, please!" God, honestly, I bet she's late tomorrow too, with more excuses.'

Fiona leant forward. 'David,' she said affectionately, 'why don't you take off your shirt?' She rose to remove his shirt very lovingly and he gave in. 'That's better. Let me see you now without these clothes…'

Despite David being skinny—and his back was becoming a little bent—his wife still found him attractive. Tonight, she had made up her mind to go to bed with him by any means.

It had been ten days since David fell ill. However, he had started to recover after his meeting with the council chairman. He had begun to regain some of his composure and sense of awareness. But his ability to focus soon drained away by the end of the evening. The cheque's affair soon took over as it began to pop up momentarily, looming in his memory. He clung to it for a while, but Fiona's quick and varied conversation seemed to dispel it and tear it apart, until the cheque alone glowed in his memory, without his being able to link it with his wife or with anybody else for that matter. He did not understand why the cheque alone was floating in his memory.

Fiona intended to divert her husband's attention and was successful, but the desire to seduce David became intense, taking hold of her and turning her on, after nights of his returning from the council, exhausted and lacking in libido. She found herself really stimulated now. The cheap wine made her tipsy and whet her appetite for sex, and stirred up David's lust and enthusiasm to respond in kind to her intoxicated passion by touching the exposed bits of her body in order to arouse her. David's coldness irritated her to such an extent that she decided to take the initiative herself putting her hand under the table and pulled down her trousers to reveal white, beautiful, provocative thighs, and desperately courting foreplay. She then laid his hand on her silky thigh, whispering, 'You haven't come near me for ten days. Haven't you been thinking of me all this time? I mean, don't you desire me?'

David remained still while she guided his hand up and down her tender thigh, then slowly placed it on her underwear while simultaneously leaning against him, kissing the side of his face and neck. She then pushed his hand down inside her panties, allowing him to tease her pubes, pressing her aroused and sensitive clitoris.

Sensing no response, she said in a tantalisingly low, raspy voice, 'Let's go to bed.'

David was dragged to the bedroom. In front of the bed, his trousers were taken off and he was made to lie down on the bed. She stretched herself out; lying beside him and pulling the bed-sheet over her legs she moved her body closer to him, burning with carnal desire. She hugged him tightly. Then her hand slithered down to his shorts, pulling them down. She held his genitalia, teasing them while keeping her body in close contact with his, gently biting his neck like a pet dog, her saliva running profusely down her teeth. She was now messaging his genitalia, moving her hand up and down, relaxing it for a moment, and a moment later frantically tightening it, whispering in a low voice, 'Come here, please! Come here, David!'

But in the end she relented, her warm hand still gripping a cold, lifeless, wrinkled lump of skin.

-3-

Finally, experts from the software company OPCAL arrived to examine the council's application. In fact, it was a single expert, short and gaunt, about twenty-five years of age, carrying an elegant Samsonite, in fact much more elegant than he was. He arrived from the capital and stayed overnight in one of the grandest hotels. He arrived on time. That morning, he sat in the secretary's room waiting to meet the council chairman.

Rose was thrown momentarily into a feverish state. She kept going out and coming back into her room without any reason. Her lower lip was bitten and swollen. A big, dry scab was turning crimson. She let Mr Hudson know that the expert had arrived. He told her to ask him to wait for two minutes while he finished what he was doing. Meanwhile, the deputy, Mr Pickard entered, holding a handkerchief. He greeted the expert and was effusive in showing his respect, then they exchanged a few words about the weather.

The expert maintained a tough, serious posture, which was not compatible with his height, he was constantly adjusting his necktie as if he had not been used to it.

After fourteen days of prodding and jogging David's faded memory, and snooping around Three Hills and spying on its inhabitants in the hope of extracting one voluntary confession relating to receiving the cheque, the council had decided to contact the company with a view to sending in experts to examine the software to find out whether the malfunction was inherent in the design of the system, or was due to the negligence of David.

The expert entered the chairman's office, followed by Mr Pickard and the secretary, swinging her posterior beneath the short skirt to some inaudible music. She closed the door behind her.

Mr Hudson the chairman—a dissipating wave of smoke floating over his head, rolling over and thickening into wick shapes, then settling on the ceiling—welcomed the expert and shook his hand. He grinned to reveal a big smile that masked the pain which had deepened the lines on his face. He smiled for any reason and no reason at all.

The expert was asked if his trip from London was comfortable. The little gentleman replied, 'It was indeed.'

Mr Hudson began in earnest. 'Does the OPCAL application need only testing, or maintenance?'

'Possibly both!' responded the expert.

The chairman cast a quick look at his deputy, then at the computer expert, and asked 'Is there any difference between the two? I would've thought each is an integral part of the other!'

The expert retorted, steadying his necktie. 'The Company has adopted a policy of testing the functionality of the application in addition to its half-yearly maintenance. Each will cost you two hundred thousand pounds.'

There was one more look from the chairman toward his deputy who shrugged, indicating that he had nothing to do with the company policy. He was only meant to pay the allocated amount and collect an invoice.

The chairman pointed out to the expert the failings of the OPCAL application, based on what David had said before his memory became flawed. The situation had brought upon the council a catastrophe that he was unable to disclose at present. 'The software,' he explained, 'does not respond appropriately to the main commands. The data disintegrates when it is requested in full. It also becomes muddled up when it is expected to appear separate. The addresses are scrambled. Town addresses are mixed up with village addresses and, therefore, it has become difficult to determine the exact statistics. Do you believe the OPCAL application is in need of testing or maintenance?'

'In that situation', said the expert, who had now sunk deeper into the soft cushion, with the secretary standing behind, not seeing him but only hearing his voice, 'as stated in the company policy, it requires testing and maintenance simultaneously. First, let's identify the root cause of this confusion, as your excellency you put it. Then we proceed with the required repairs. That will cost the council four hundred thousand pounds.'

The deputy's eyes flew towards the window when the chairman shot him a look from the corner of his eye. His handkerchief incessantly wiping away the beads of perspiration from his face and double chin. Meanwhile, the secretary's eyes remained spellbound on the slender figure of the chairman, undressing it and hugging it with fatal passion.

A moment passed in silence. Then the council chairman gave the expert the go-ahead to start the testing and maintenance of the software.

The three-man procession left, the expert and his Samsonite briefcase walking ahead, followed by the deputy and Mrs Bennet. Her eyes clung closely to the chairman, her posterior swinging provocatively, pleadingly, seeking to seduce Mr Hudson and catch his downcast eyes. He was, however, engrossed in the new figures that had taken him unaware, upsetting his calculations.

When they had left and the door was closed, the chairman took a long list of austerity measures from the drawer and laid it in front of him. He mulled it over once again, amending the numbers on the right, changing the overall outcome and doubling the amount. He reflected upon it. He believed it was still insufficient.

He wasted a significant part of the morning, crossing out, altering and adding, until his coffee, prepared by Rose, became cold. This prompted her to keep asking, her yearning heightened, if he wanted another coffee.

'No', he replied absent-mindedly, chasing accounts, imploring them to relinquish more, while the white smoke, as seen by Rose, shot in straight lines from his ears, like the haloes of prophets, floating upwards, only to settle finally beneath the ceiling.

Half an hour later, the three-man procession returned. First came the expert, then the deputy, with Rose, trailing behind them, she closed the door.

The council chairman stowed away his list, which was covered in crosses, in the drawer and regained his senses.

The expert began by saying, 'We have completed our tests and repairs.' He then produced a bill, which the deputy took out and passed on with a shaking hand to the chairman. The expert continued, 'The OPCAL application is running like a Swiss watch. But...'

'But what?' The council chairman as if he was coming out of a reverie.

'OPCAL has designed a new version of the application that suits you perfectly.' From his Samsonite briefcase he produced a disc. 'A new version that suits the coordinated and cross-referenced confidential data relevant to the residents, and the affairs of towns and villages, compatible with the speed of your system. The data will leap across the screen at high speed!'

He displayed the disc like an icon that had just fallen from the sky.

All eyes were transfixed by the new copy, the divine icon, hoisted as high as the arm of the expert could stretch. Silence and trepidation prevailed.

'And... how much will this new copy cost us?' the council chairman asked.

'The company is offering it at the same price as the old copy, two hundred thousand pounds,' responded the expert, slipping the copy back into the bag still wide open across his knees.

'And why did you carry out the test and the

maintenance, that cost the council four hundred thousand pounds, if we were to pay two hundred thousand pounds for the new copy?' The chairman tried to outsmart the expert while simultaneously suppressing the bitter fury that was about to erupt.

'A very important question,' the expert responded. 'You can choose not to buy it, but the company will stop supporting the old version of the software, and you will find yourself lagging behind and compelled to buy it next year in order to keep up with the latest updates of the applications that will later be introduced by the company!'

'In the name of all gods, ancient and modern, how am I supposed to understand this conundrum?' asked the chairman, glancing sideways at the deputy who shrugged, implying he did not understand the company's philosophy. He was secretly satisfied, though, with the anticipated rise in its share prices.

Meanwhile, standing at the back, Rose, her longing and passion soaring and subsiding with the rise and fall of his temper, was ready to answer any call, big or small, from Mr Hudson, that would bring solace to her long-suffering heart.

The expert demonstrated a unique skill in explaining and re-explaining the company's policy and pricing. He went on to elaborate on what was an obvious yet, twisted statement in his estimation of the speed of the new version and the benefits to be reaped by the council if they purchased it, underestimating the price which was not a lot, in comparison with the merits of OPCAL after the new modifications and additions. He swore on his professional honour that he alone had sold two thousand copies in the last period. From her position at the back of the room, Rose could see nothing of the sinking expert. She could only hear a tongue articulating from a record placed on a small coffee table. Typical salesman! Brainy hypocrite!

The council chairman agreed to pay the amount, without comprehending anything that had been said. His deputy was all smiles and the 'machine' stopped talking.

When the expert left, followed by the buoyant deputy who was drowned in sweat and ecstasy, Rose closed the door. The council chairman placed in front of him sheets of papers filled with crossing-outs, murmuring to himself that a portion of the funds allocated for the computer programs ought to be added to the austerity list, and another part to the percentage imposed on the companies. He went on making amendments, crossing out and adding, until the list began to resemble Google's aerial map.

Filing the council budgets used to be fairly easy. They did not warrant the fury of the council chairman; rather, they required his composure and focus. Some addition here; some deletion there. Then the budget would regain its former state, as outlined by the government—after deducting the surplus which is the chairman's.

But the unpredictable, painful blow experienced by the Three Hills had shaken Mr Hudson's self-confidence and caused his heart to bleed. What is Three Hills, after all? It is a cursed town. It had been upgraded to the rank of town due to the increase in its birth rate. He vowed to be revenged on the town until the ten million unfairly taken out of his account had been returned.

He pressed the secretary's button. She came in immediately and was told to re-type the list. Once she had finished typing it, she needed to bring it along with the deputy, Pickard, to him. Meanwhile, he stared out the window, laden with worry, missing a glimpse of Mrs Bennet's buttocks.

The chairman thought about the administrative staff, the technical staff and the skilled workers attached to the council but who worked outside it. They were on the council's books. Their number, not known with absolute certainty, exceeded the capacity of the budget. Why was there a vast number of employees allocated to serve citizens and deal with their daily inquiries? Why were committees set up to monitor other committees, to ascertain the legality of their measures?

What was the point of collecting rubbish each week when rubbish bags could be tightly secured, awaiting fortnightly collection instead?

The council chairman was preoccupied with how to reduce the number of workers and services to a level adequate enough to satisfy the regulations.

Perhaps government performance would not be paralysed should an employee or employees be sent back home to look after their children. particularly since Downing Street often turn to be a brick wall when it came to one or two complaints made by people.

-4-

Fiona was frustrated and on the verge of despair after ten days of grappling with the shrunken lump of skin, which turned lifeless in her warm hand.

She began brooding over the distressing nights in which she flirted but to no avail. She wondered if she had lost David forever as a husband, and as a man who warmed her bed and filled it with fervent panting and desire upon feeling her nakedness, so that every part of his body hardened in response. 'There's no use! Not even a glimmer of hope!'

She reminisced while her scissors clipped away her customers' hair, chasing her thoughts; rather, chasing solutions to her recent ordeal which inflicted pain and suffering upon her marital life. She remembered her desperate attempts last night when she kissed David, whispering words of passion to send blood and warmth into his member. She bent before him and over him. She tried every provocative sexual position, but the "foreskin" remained lifeless, shrivelled, warning Fiona to expect very cold nights.

'But no!' she said to herself, 'David will recover from this health issue and regain his sexual energy', and the projection she thought too small was, nevertheless, encouraging if she knew where to start.

What is an erection? How does it happen, and why does it fail?

She went into the small library, adjacent to the newsagent's shop in Three Hills. She began by reading the published research papers and articles on the Internet, in the salon. She concluded that three factors contributed to erectile dysfunction. Firstly, when a man reached the age of sixty. Secondly, if he came down with diabetes. Neither condition applied to David. He was twenty-eight and was free of all diseases. He certainly didn't have diabetes. The third factor was the fracturing of the pelvis in an accident. This was also ruled out in David's case.

But, how did erection, turn Fiona's days into misery, throwing her life into the unknown, come about?

Studies indicate and in the forefront the incidence of sexual stimulation, which Fiona excels at displaying, but to no avail. Next came the inability of the member to achieve hardness that would enable it to penetrate the vagina, a condition called 'sagging'. When Fiona was young, she used to join in with the other women in their discussion of sagging, cracking jokes about it. Little did she predict that it would one day become her daily concern, something she would not be able to divulge.

After reviewing all the studies and none of them applied to David's general health, the methods suggested for restoring erection to its former natural state were ointments and injections, arterial surgery, reconstructive surgery, and, should all the aforementioned remedies fail, a 'member' transplant was recommended.

'Oh my God!' Fiona let out a cry in front of the computer as if she had just received a mighty blow to her forehead. When one of the salon assistants asked:

'What's the matter, Fiona?' one of the salon assistants asked.

She replied, feigning a smile, 'Nothing! Just a silly joke on the Internet.'

She frowned and muttered to herself, 'Replacing a "member" by another.' She wondered who would donate his own penis? Body parts transplants had become one of the most advanced inventions of modern medicine and all operations had been successful.

If medicine had been successful in transplanting the heart, the kidney and the eye, why not a penis? She thought David might not object if she chose the right one for herself. It was down to him, but she was ultimately the one concerned; particularly when it came to the length of the 'member', its smoothness, its coarseness and its girth as well. She recalled that she sometimes wished, at the moment of eroticism, that if only the length of David's penis was to extend a few centimetres to quench her thirst for more. Her thoughts travelled down to her lower abdomen. She visualized her pudendum. She admitted that David was doing his best during foreplay, but his 'member' could hardly touch or massage all the edges of her vagina in equal measure. If only she could try a 'member' that would fill up her pudendum, slipping inside and simultaneously rubbing every part to its entry.

She ruminated while holding the computer's mouse tightly, imagining it to be a healthy, erect penis that belonged to David, squeezing it in her hand, feeling its heat and raging hardness, guiding the compliant dick to her vagina to penetrate her. She felt some sweet moistness oozing, then spreading across the lips of her pudendum in her knickers. A moment later, she came out of her reverie to close the research page quickly, before she was spotted by one of the assistants, who would her out of curiosity ask why she was reading about 'erection'. She, however, kept the site's appointments page on.

When she got up, the door opened to reveal a young woman with her straight hair, dyed red, lifted and upwardly scattered. She was wearing a hot mini skirt, so tight that her behind stood out, fully showing her thighs. Dangling from her shoulders, a red handbag matching the colour of her hair. She was carrying a small, tatty suitcase, which she dumped on the floor. She waited for Fiona who saw the advancing face, blurred by the glare of the sun, beaming from the street, to identify her. The sun behind her made it difficult for Fiona to see her face.

'Hi Fiona!' the young girl greeted her, and Fiona recognised the voice of her sister.

'Hi Ruth' Fiona luke-warmly replied, as she was taken by surprise, then was struck dumb.

Ruth dragged the suitcase away from the door and entered the salon. She exchanged a frosty kiss with her elder sister. The two assistants greeted her as they would any customer. They had never met Ruth before. They were not surprised by her appearance as the salon attracted various types of customers. Ruth sat on the chair next to the door and picked up a magazine, leafing through it without focusing. When Fiona asked if she had gone round to see her mother and her husband she said 'No' without even lifting her eyes from the page. She tossed the magazine back onto the pile, a thin smile appearing on her pretty face throughout.

Fiona avoided maintaining direct eye contact with her, pretending to be pre-occupied with trivial issues in the salon, often sneaking a look apprehensively, worried, trying to get to the bottom of the reason why she came back, to put her through yet another ordeal no doubt.

Ruth is contentious, never on good terms with anyone. She does not think before she speaks. Her enduring smile masks her disgust with everything around her. All her acquaintances presume that that smile is given shape by a disfigurement, no more no less, as it contradicts the disorder in her psyche. As for her, she turns around, taking the analysis with a smile and stays away since she has always found everything easily accessible in her life. Therefore she is always on the lookout for something new, setting her apart from the rest.

Ruth left Three Hills four years ago. She spent all that time in the capital. In the early years she would come back to her mother's house, then leave again, thrown out as usual, due to her defiance. At times she left of her own accord, self-evicted after a row or a fiery argument. She would often end up at the railway station in the town if she happened to have the train fare or bus station in Three Hills. She would sit all day, waiting for someone to lend her money or she would beg off for it, and sometimes even fall in love with whoever paid her fare. She would then disappear and no one would hear from her again; that is, until she was ready.

During the last four years Three Hills had become used to Ruth's continual absence and heaved a collective sigh of relief. Her absence troubled no one. As a sixteen-year-old who left home for the first time, she generated in her wake a dust trail of arguments, problems and fear, till she reached the age when she was in control of her own destiny; thus, burying fury, violence and her family's former concerns, which she pushed behind, where accumulated events were consigned to memory alone.

Now, past experience and Ruth's sudden resurrection threw Fiona into a dilemma. She could neither force her into going to her mother, as her mother and particularly her husband 'her stepfather', had both grown fed up with Ruth and pushed her out of their minds since that time, nor take her to her own house because she would stir up troubles. Besides, she had David's problems to deal with, and she had not the slightest idea how long Ruth was going to stay.

After Fiona locked up the salon, Ruth walked with her as though she was accepting an unspoken invitation. It was taken for granted and both seemed resigned to it. Once at home, they found themselves facing each other at the kitchen dining table. Fiona asked why she had returned, having carved a life for herself elsewhere.

'I need some money!' Ruth answered, still wearing a smile.

'Money?' Fiona asked in astonishment. 'I thought you were never short of money, considering what you do for a living!'

'I will never come back to Three Hills again if you give me some money to start life anew!' said Ruth, settling the matter once and for all in her own charming way, busying herself, twiddling her fingers or biting her nails, looking at Fiona, maintaining her smile throughout.

'Money? David's job and mine combined can hardly pay the rent, bills, taxes and the necessities of life. Where would I get the money from?

'What about the ten thousand pounds?' asked Ruth, blowing up what Fiona had been suppressing and waiting for a reaction.

'What?' Fiona was panic stricken.

Ruth was unabashed with her naive approach and audacious argument with her sister. But the revelation of this secret in such a direct manner transformed Fiona into a ferocious cat, baring her teeth and claws. Fiona confronted her sister with a fierce, darting look. Then she retreated and the severity left her eyes. Finally, she asked, with eyes downcast, 'How did you know?'

'I just know,' replied Ruth, with a smile which Fiona found repulsive and disgusting.

‘I will not give you any of this money,’ she said after thinking for a while. ‘It is all we have. Besides, the government might be alerted and demand it back. The matter hasn’t been determined yet. It’s all we have now.’

‘Don’t be silly. The government doesn’t want to take it back!’

‘Oh, no?’ Fiona wondered, sarcastically. ‘The government will skin you down to the bone once they find out there’s an error. What do you think they’re going to do?’

‘I don’t care what they do. Just give me some of it. I want to pay off my debts and buy some clothes,’ said Ruth.

‘Debts? What about the money you made from your dirty profession? We didn’t ask you to help us with money. Why do you want us to pay off your debts now?’ Fiona snapped.

‘Calm down!’ Ruth begged of her sister.

‘We’re embarrassed by the neighbours’ queries and looks.’ Fiona became more vehement, capitulating on the new situation.

‘I am not the only one doing this, you know. There are thousands, in fact, millions of girls and women like me!’ countered Ruth quietly, unperturbed.

‘Your reputation has sunk to the lowest level,’ sniffed Fiona.

‘I don’t care. I can do whatever I want with my body!’

She added after a moment of silence, 'I did it twice, and after that they stopped calling me.'

Fiona retorted sarcastically, 'Twice! On video and on the Internet! How naive are you? People will be talking about you all your life, whether it is two, or twenty times, don't you know that? You open your thighs wide for men to view on the Internet and the whole of England will watch you gyrate shamelessly!' She then turned her face away.

'I have told you, I don't care. Are you going to give me some of what you've collected?'

Ruth had an unsavoury past. She had wandered around the capital and mixed with a group of unemployed young people, the marginalised and the beggars. When she was just eighteen, she was picked up by a video artist. He took her to a room with a bed and a shower and persuaded her to shoot a video featuring her having sex with a man, to be shown on specific sites on the Internet, promising her a thousand pounds for every clip.

Ruth had to admit that she found her role immensely pleasurable at first. She took off her clothes and learnt the provocative positions, under and on top of a man, how to pant and gasp and groan in response to the photographer's direction, how to draw his fullness into the tightness between her legs, and then into her mouth and anus. When the filming was over, she watched hundreds of Internet sites where naked women and young girls smiled at the camera, culminating in a display of explicit sex. Her film was later shown on the small screen, but she noticed that the man hid his face. Only his massive penis was showing, ready to perform its desired role.

The photographer proclaimed that she would be a well-known porn star after loading the film. She was delighted. But, in the end, she felt nauseous where the penis had gone deep inside her mouth, and intense pain lingered in her anus. The photographer gave her five hundred pounds and got rid of her after the second film. Repetition, he thought, however skilful the girl might be, was the deadly enemy of such films.

Ruth stared at her bewildered sister, determined to get her hands on some of the money. Fiona kept quiet about it, determined not to touch the ten thousand pounds, thinking of a peaceful way to throw her sister out. Better still; her sister might get tired of waiting and leave.

She alerted her to David's illness and warned her against harassing him, but she kept his sexual condition well hidden from her.

-5-

Rose Bennet sat in her office, thinking and thinking all over again of the council chairman's ignoring her, of his neglect and pretence to be busy, which he unabashedly continued to display toward her! She swore she would use all means to drag Hudson by his shirt to the storeroom even though it was midday, to live and die in his arms and moist thighs, panting underneath him; lying by his side until her sexual thirst, starved out of sex for over a month, was quenched. A month whose days were filled with unbridled sexual appetite circling around it and whose fervent nights were spent away from the trigger for her lust.

She had managed yesterday to decode the enigma of the ten thousand pounds through David himself. She sat alone with him in his guarded office and was able to draw from him a confession. Her big mouth opened, teeth bared in dry amusement, ominously warning of serious things to come. She was determined that such a trifling matter should not stop Hudson from frequenting the shrine.

In the morning, she confronted the staff with excuses, preventing them from going in to see the council chairman for any reason, even if it was essential. He was 'busy' with more important issues. She then pasted a small 'Do not disturb the Chairman while reviewing budget' sign on the door. Later, she treated everyone indifferently, choosing to beckon to them to observe the sign on the door in answer to their urgent demands to see or consult the chairman, collecting the letters and documents brought in and putting them on her desk for the attention of the chairman as required.

Her passion-inflamed mind rambled in search of plans that would lure him to the shrine. Chief among them was the appointment she had fixed for the TEF pharmaceutical company's sales representative. She was aware of Hudson's thirty per cent commission for facilitating the monopoly of their drug sales to towns and villages within the regional boundaries of the municipality. Thus Rose would be able to sneak her way into his blissful heart and take him into the shrine, as in the delightful, good old days, after every successful transaction.

The clock struck three, alerting all her senses, when the sales representative made his entrance on time. She stood up to welcome him, and her facial contraction instantly breaking into smiles. She then tapped her fingers twice on the door, rhythmically, and entered, followed by the sales representative, who carried a briefcase replete with documents. She introduced him in a loud voice, 'The sales representative of TEF pharmaceutical company is here to see you, sir.'

Mr Hudson showed particular interest in the sales representative. He complimented the pharmaceutical company and declared that the citizens preferred buying its products over those of other companies. Rose retained her position behind the sales deputy in anticipation of any request. Meanwhile, the chairman kept sneaking a look at her, alerting her to disappear, as he was about to discuss the percentage. This subject required thorough discussion and finalisation too, away from the eavesdroppers, particularly her and her idiotic habit of listening in on his conversations. However, despite the fleeting nature, she was enjoying what she believed were his glances at her mini skirt and bare legs, for him and him alone. Glances met with her own sly smiles.

'How about a cup of tea for the sales representative?' said Mr Hudson directing his words at the secretary, shattering her fantasies. 'Oh, certainly, Mr Hudson!' She sauntered into the storeroom cum kitchenette, swinging her buttocks merrily.

After pressing the kettle with a tick, she inspected the bed, gently stroking the double pillow with eagerness. She smoothed the bed sheets again, as she did every morning. 'He will not get away from me today!' she murmured to herself, promising herself that she would put an end to this brutal deprivation, moving, in circles, around Hudson, sniffing his scent during the day, tossing and turning during the night.

She re-adjusted her clothes, pressed her hands against her buttocks as though they were Hudson's hands. She lifted her skirt to expose as much of her legs as possible, taking stock of her shirt, pressing her breasts slightly together, making sure to show the white flesh of her cleavage, sliding down from her sultry neck to the top of her supple breasts.

'Where do I start gobbling the tasty duck?' she said, copying him. She attributed the smoke rising from his head to self-deprivation, amidst family obligations and worries, preventing him from rolling in her open arms. Nothing as trivial as ten thousand pounds going to Three Hills's inhabitants! The government was quite capable of clawing back the amount pence by pence. All he had to do was alert the government to the error and they would know what to do.

Tick. The kettle reached boiling point and she prepared two cups of milky tea. Before she took them to the office, she took a final look, content with her appearance. She brushed her chest for the third time with perfume, then took in every detail of the storeroom, visualising its full readiness to embrace them. Then she carried the tea on a beautiful tray and left.

Mr Hudson had already struck a deal with the TEF sales representative, stipulating that a forty per cent commission would be paid in return for the company's monopoly of all sales in town and villages attached to the council. They rose to shake hands, looking very pleased with themselves.

At the beginning, neither would budge on fifty per cent, considering the huge risks. Another company renowned for its effective drugs had offered Mr

Hudson fifty per cent, without too much haggling.

'Thirty per cent,' insisted the sales representative. Talking about effectiveness is irrelevant in the drugs industry since the company sells headache medicine that causes stomach perforations, then promotes a drug for the stomach causing hypertension; then another drug to lower blood pressure, leading to the accumulation of potassium in the body. It operates like a saw, cutting as it goes downwards and cutting as it goes up. TEF was facing a sharp decline in the annual profit margin as a result of the external competition facing local drug companies. 'Do you want me to give you numbers, your Excellency Mr Chairman?'

'No, I am not interested in these numbers. *My* numbers say I have paid ten million pounds from my own personal account because of the behaviour of a stupid employee. Fifty per cent is commensurate with your monopoly in our region.' replied Mr. Hudson.

A puff of smoke went upwards. The mere mention of the ten thousand pounds or Three Hills caused the smoke to rise from his head, like a steamboat sailing along the Thames.

'Let's say forty-five and drop anchor at an agreement!' added the council chairman, as he was leaning back in his chair.

'Let's say thirty five. I'm not authorised to offer a higher payment.' came the quick sales representative's response.

Eventually, after much haggling, they agreed on forty per cent, and the council chairman rose to his feet and extended his hand. The sales representative rose from his seat to shake the extended hand.

At that very moment Rose came out of the storeroom carrying the tea tray. She was surprised to see the two men smiling, bracing hands in agreement. The council chairman then strode towards the door, bidding the sales deputy goodbye, returning to his office with a slow, happy and confident step.

Rose placed the tray on the nearest table. Happiness glowed across her powder-smudged face. She quickly headed for the office door, brought the key inside and locked herself and the chairman in. She turned to the council chairman, pulling him by the shirt into the storeroom, giving him no chance to think, repeating, 'Come, take me, for heaven's sake!'

It was midday. She took off all his clothes while he feigned resistance, simultaneously, wishing to stop her, but to no avail.

'Have you gone mad?' he repeatedly whispered, in rhythm with the falling to the floor of every piece of his or her clothing, until they were left naked. Sticking and clinging to him she gasped, 'Take me! I'm dying with desire.'

They flung themselves together on the sofa bed.

After their legs were entwined in an embrace, she stretched out a hand for a glass of whisky she had already prepared. He drank a generous mouthful, then she put it back on the table, panting with overwhelming desire.

Her feverish hands pressed against his back, feeling his nakedness, her mouth kissing, her thighs squeezing and her tongue deliciously hot.

'Take me… Take me.'

And he responded to her, pressing her body against his. His senses were awakening. He felt the wetness flowing her pudendum, sticky, flowing over his thighs.

He mustered all his powers to respond favourably to her blessed, blazing passion, but she felt, with her belly and tender-skinned legs, that something was missing from the raging duel.

She extended her hand downwards, feeling his prick with her warm hand, and realised it was a shrunken, shrivelled skin, unresponsive to her frantic pleas.

She stretched her body under his torso and let her mouth do the work, kissing it, lightly biting it with the tips of her teeth and taking it all in. She sucked it, her saliva no less sticky than the saliva profusely secreted by her pudendum. Yet it refused to get up, remaining cold and maintaining its shrinkage.

'What?' she asked, looking at him from below with startled eyes. 'What happened to him?' she asked again. Her tense nerves began to loosen up. Her hand still holding the tip, close to her gaping mouth, saliva flowing from the corner, her bare posterior radiant under the silver light. She waited for an explanation from his eyes. Eyes not long ago overflowing with lust, now staring at the ceiling. Waiting for him to explain the catastrophe that had befallen his member, like a lovesick mermaid, pleading with her worshipped god for his maritime intercession, before her supple body dried up.

'I can't', he replied in a subdued voice, his eyes still nailed to the ceiling.

He was incapable, though he desired her. He made an effort, yet he failed. His dick, still in her hand, a mere shrunken, droopy worm, utterly helpless, incurable. There was no trace of stiffness, no swelling of arteries. She lifted it in her hand, pushing it forward, willing to partake in foreplay before penetration.

He hid from her his bitter nightly hell, in which all sexual attempts with his wife ended in unspeakable failure. They rolled over on the bed, with him staring at the ceiling, as now, and his wife looking in despair at his blonde pubic hair and his reclining member that resembled a wilted plant against his pink thigh.

Defeated, he enlisted his wife's help with efforts to change his diet, to diversify into different foods, fortifying it with added vitamins so that he might be able to fulfil his matrimonial obligations.

Neither eggs and honey nor cured meat for breakfast was of any use. Neither foul red meat nor slices of calf and hot sauce, served with fine wine for supper, was able to breathe life into his prick and make it stand upright.

Neither essential oils nor strong arousers, nor massaging his testicles and thighs and upper groin, with his wife displaying, sometimes, shameful sexual positions to facilitate the erection of the council chairman's member.

The doctor was not surprised by the chairman's condition, which seemed out of keeping with his youth, physical strength and sound health. He gave the couple a smile and made light of the catastrophic feeling that overwhelmed them, because patients with sexual frustration in England represented one in ten men and women. They suffered from impotence because they were under psychological pressure; or, rather, what is called the modern lifestyle, feelings of guilt, nervousness, worry and depression. Tens of men and women, in their prime, visited him every day, all with the same problem. He advised local injections as a quick solution, coupled with assistance by the wife in the arousal process, using her hand, or her mouth, if necessary, to facilitate the erection.

In case of failure, he advised that they returned to him to try a new drug about to be launched on the market, because companies, meaning drug companies, give impotence the necessary commercial attention!

Rose the secretary, however, would not stop at

doctors and specialists. She plunged deeper into her pessimistic obsessions. She went in her Volkswagen to see a group of gypsies who were camping nearby and spent half a day among their tattered caravans, in search of those concerned with the care of the prick, curing erectile dysfunction with magic or herbal remedies. She was led by a group of men and children, circling the mobile homes. They eventually took her to see a grey-haired hag. The withered woman led her inside her putrid caravan and sat her on an upside-down jerry can, in front of what looked like a disturbed laboratory: glass bottles, pipes, a beaker puffing out steam, reminding her of the curling smoke over Hudson's head. She said to her: 'Tell me about your crisis with the prick, my dear.'

6

During Ruth's first week at Fiona's house, the latter wouldn't budge an inch on her position concerning the money. She wouldn't offer any amount, however small it was in Ruth's opinion, because she feared it would be taken as a sign of giving in, which would encourage her to come to Three Hills whenever she needed money. Ruth's pressing habit resembled the relation between the hive and the bees, with the difference that the bees' return added benefits, while Ruth's took and wasted.

Fiona, for her part, had a little place, a little corner of her heart filled with affection for her sister. She remembered her sister at the age of three, pretty with long hair and two small, emerald eyes that smiled as she carried and teased her. Therefore, she decided to ignore her faults and sins and not throw her out on the first day. Poor Ruth didn't know how to handle her life. She mixed with life's losers. She rebelled against her mother. Her own mother cut off the kinship for a daughter she does not know well enough, and never considered her own future as a woman.

Ruth made herself homeless very early, went hungry, slept in every bed that offered food and warmth for one or a couple of nights. She was convinced she had the right to loot all she could lay hands on, in order to survive like the rest of humanity, and rats and dogs and monkeys, whether it came from her sister, or a sex-hungry shark, or a loner looking for companionship. As long as this house offered food, light and a bed, she would remain in it until she got what she wanted!

The warm water poured from the shower over Ruth's naked body. Today was Saturday and Fiona left for the salon in haste since people had begun spending the council's money generously on their appearance, and men and women were desperate for appointments. Fiona wasn't about to grumble. Business was great.

Fiona noted that the women, even the old ones, had begun arriving one after the other to have their faces looked after, have their hair dyed, and their neglected eyebrows waxed. Fiona and the assistants began working overtime to cope with the demand of customers who were standing in a queue outside the salon that was too busy to accommodate them. Fiona would return home exhausted. She would have supper and go to bed immediately, too weak to argue over what was right and wrong regarding her money, the council's money.

Ruth left the bathroom exuding fragrances of soap and shampoo. She dried her white body, the taut body of the young in all its beautiful detail.

Her dyed hair had reverted to its natural blonde, free of the dye reminiscent of hippies. Her emerald eyes emerged from their deep sockets, giving prominence to two rosy cheeks that became full when she smiled her familiar smile.

She rummaged through the contents of her tatty kingdom. The suitcase was her companion in her days of fortune and misfortune. Very often, she would be thrown out of doors, totally ignored by passersby. Ruth would swear and curse in a loud voice. She would walk a few steps, only to remember her suitcase and go back to pick it up off the street.

She was left it by a young traveller. They had spent the night at Victoria railway station. When he woke up on the bench, he realised his train was due to depart in one minute. He ran towards his compartment, only to remember his bag. He turned around to shout out, 'Keep it for yourself!'

When she opened it, she found nothing in it apart from a pair of tattered trousers, a toothbrush, and a book that had lost its cover, with its initial pages ripped out. It was about tourism in India. She kept the book, turned the bag upside down and emptied the rest of the contents into the rubbish bin. Then she placed in it her belongings, which she was carrying along with the book pages in a cloth bag, and went back to sleep.

Ruth left David sound asleep, though it was getting late. because she knew that Saturday was for sleeping in, for employees and non-employees, and David was good for nothing, anyway. She remembered from her childhood days when she used to come to Fiona's house, he was withdrawn and did not talk much. He used to ask her about her lessons, questions about geography which she excelled in.

'What is the capital of Finland?' and 'Where is Kenya located?'

But he would quickly become fed up and ignore her for the rest of the time, losing himself in thoughts no one knew anything about.

'Those who run after their thoughts, actually try to mask what is already widespread among the people, but I don't care' she said to herself, picking up the red-handled bag and went out. She knew Sales Street, on which Fiona's house was situated, very well. It ended, after a few more houses, in a cul-de-sac. She neither noticed its many potholes nor realised how overwhelmingly chaotic it was.

In her early days she used to retire to a room at home to read the India book and by night, she used to walk about Three Hills, looking around its streets and shops since she was absent for four years, which felt like four centuries that cast their ancient shadow over the valley, its houses and its streets, which she had walked in her childhood and adolescence, hand-span by hand-span, for it was here started wandering off.

She turned toward Cleanliness Street, looking with a smile at the puddle that blocked her way. Could it have been the continual rain of the previous days that had created this tiny sea?

Directly opposite, a middle-aged woman appeared, carrying grocery bags, wading in the water, grumbling and cursing, feeling her way with caution. Before she entered one of the houses, she shouted out, 'Take the other street if you wish to avoid getting wet, and pray that the council may live to a ripe old age, so that many more sewage pipes may burst!'

Still smiling, Ruth made a detour towards The Happy Days Street, where the water was a little shallower, easier to skip over, or walk along its edges.

When Three Hills was built randomly and in haste, half a century ago, the engineers were faced with the problem of choosing names for its streets.

Apart from the runway which ran through the middle of the town and earned the nomenclature 'Sticky Trap', a legacy left by the British Army, the cartographers who drew the earliest map for the village that expanded to become a town were puzzled as to how to choose names for the roads branching out from the main street and climbing the surrounding hills.

One of the engineers had a novel idea, harmonious with the standard of work, on the one hand, and the wishes and dreams of the owners of the houses, on the other. Therefore, they allowed the new residents to choose the names of the streets on which their houses would rise in accordance with their wishes and dreams of opulence.

The Three Hills residents, in a buoyant mood, assembled and chose the names that befitted their dreams and outlooks on a new life, entirely different from the village and city life lived by their fellow English folk. For instance, the Happy Days Street, along which Ruth was hopping like a kangaroo to avoid the pits and puddles, was representative of people's choices at that time. It was a name which expressed their aspirations and what they were promised. This was also true of Prosperity Street and Safe Houses. Some residents summed up their hopes in their choice of 'Fair Fare' for a street name. Others were so optimistic and upbeat that they called their street 'Fair Taxes Street'.

While it is true that urban history and heritage is not free from the incidence of names reoccurring in most towns, and still retain their shine in people's mind and imagination, people are, nevertheless, naturally prone to believe equally, in little and big promises, in a naive fashion, which is typical of the residents of Three Hills, with their delusions of prosperity!

Ruth had typically become consumed with the idea of spending the day cruising her childhood and teenage fairytale ground. She was the effigy of death amongst the living. She would go wherever her muck-contaminated feet took her!

Jumping over the pits was a source of delight to Ruth. The wider the hole, the bigger the challenge. Smiling like a little girl, she mustered the agility of her legs to launch herself to the other side. With this exercise, she retrieved the rapid, in-flight sensation that always sent a tremor through her body, a reminder of her childhood playtime.

In the capital, if you took one step forward you were likely to bump against someone who would scowl at you, or otherwise punch you on the nose.

The pungent smell stifled her, the stench given off by the piled-up rubbish bags, left uncollected for the last three weeks. There were overflowing wheelie bins and waste littered on the ground. The scene triggered a succession of memories. She covered her nose. The smell of the cut-up uterus on the table in front of her; her black, blood-smeared fingers; the sticky, mucous liquid and the bloodied pair of scissors, shearing off the placenta and the peritoneum will rise as high as her stretched arm, to strike at her mutilated guts.

A young surgeon agreed to perform the operation in return for keeping the uterus for medical experiments. She went back to the hospital and fished it out of the formaldehyde and left.

'No more giving birth after today!' she was saying to herself, a lifeless smile appearing on her lips.

'This piece is for Becky, so that she may not contemplate giving birth, and that one is for Angela, lest she should have a disfigured offspring!'

Her delicate fingers were stained and covered in blood and sticky liquid. Though the uterus had a rancid, disgusting smell, this did not deter her from cutting it up, sorting out and allocating portions to the girls whose names kept popping up haphazardly in her memory, girls she had met by chance on the street. Others materialised in her life of homelessness only to disappear later. She had affection for some of them, but that did not amount to much.

And she, Ruth, asleep in the attic, was awakened by the fight breaking out downstairs, and a baby crying.

The sharp-edged scissors sliced through the remaining, contaminated, flabby mass, dissecting the flesh and the bloodied pieces divided in front of her on the table. 'And this big piece for you, Tania. It's better for you to be barren for the rest of your life, rather than receiving blows to your nose!'

And the newborn was crying and wailing on the floor. Its features were odd and deformed; a human head, with limbs resembling those of a paralysed monkey.

Frank hit Tania on the nose and demanded that she leave. He told her to go to hell with the baby that was still crying, as if denouncing its deformity, for which the mother was blamed. Repeatedly struck on her already bloodied nose, with Frank yelling out in denial, 'He's not mine!'

He pushed her toward the door to dump her on the street, along with the baby who filled the house with his howls—a waterfall of cascading cries, louder than Tania's.

'Here's a bit of my uterus, effective enough to put an end to everything. And this is for Fiona who dreams of conceiving a baby which she will shield with her chest against physical deformities!'

'From his *facon de parler*, Ruth realised, he wanted to throw Tania out in order to keep me in the little house to sleep with him. As long as the house was in his name, he was forever scheming and executing.

'This piece is for Jill, to be on her guard. Giving birth shall not prevail thereafter. Women shall not become mere wombs and pouches to take in the accursed seeds.'

She turned toward Prosperity Street, having regained her poise, banishing the uterus from her mind. The idea of going to India flashed into her imagination, taking possession of it. 'I want to go to India', she whispered to herself, as though she was addressing Fiona, 'to be amongst the needy, the crippled, until I become one of them!'

She stopped outside the nursery. Nothing had changed. The paint was peeling off. The coloured drawings of the trees, houses, Mickey Mouse and flowers had already faded away.

'India is the answer!' Her mind was made up.

She visualized her mother bringing her to the nursery every morning, holding her hand. The rest of the children arrived successively with their mothers and fathers, chattering like birds, carrying their lunch packs of sandwiches and fruit, to be received by the teachers at the door. They knew the names of all the boys and girls. She could feel the taste and pleasure of white bread with butter and eggs, or slices of cured bacon. She would bid her goodbye in the end, but her mum's perfume would linger in her nostrils. The class teacher welcomed her, placing a hand on her back and coaxing her gently inside. The children's cries mingled with that of Tania's child, pushing the nursery vision away, replacing it with that of Tania and the disjointed uterus. She walked away, dragging her feet, her head overwhelmed by the volume of shouts, screams and the squabble of children.

She was unable to shake off the reminiscence. It recurred every time she smelt an overpowering stench, or heard a child cry. It mingled with whatever visualization of screaming she might have.

She walked on silently, head bowed, watching for the potholes on the road. The rubbish bags followed her on both sides, their stench in pursuit, turning her bright morning into an exposed cemetery where the dead had risen from their graves with all their putrefaction.

She was passed by children on their way to the football pitch. One of them was holding a football against his chest with one hand, while scoring an imaginary goal with his right foot into the back of an imaginary net. The rest laughed mirthfully, joining in with the fantasy. Plodding along in their wake was a short boy, ruminating, cherishing a little thought. Curious, she stopped to ask him, 'Which team are you?'

'Dynamo Three Hills.' The child stopped to reply, raising his head, wide eyed, anticipating her surprise.

'Who are you playing today?'

'The Torch!' he said.

'Undoubtedly, you will beat them, eh?'

'I don't know!' Then he remembered to add, 'We have a brilliant goalkeeper.'

'Good luck!' she said to him, smiling.

'Thanks!' He ran to catch up with his team.

She turned to enter Paradise Street which was no different from the rest of the streets, with puddles, potholes and rubbish. However, the number of pedestrians had increased because it led to Sticky Trap Street in the centre of town.

She was convinced she would never regret the hysterectomy, as Fiona thought. Once any child grew up, he would give his wife a heavy slap on the nose, or smash the head of an old person just to steal twenty pounds that would buy him a shot of heroin. Even if the uterus grew back she would cut it up again. 'I will not present this world with any more children!' she said. 'Give me one thousand pounds! I have decided to go to India,' she addressed an imaginary Fiona, who was sitting opposite to her. 'I will not need any more than that. I will live there among the poor, until my own clothes wear out and fall to pieces, leaving me naked amongst them. There, I will not be in need of clothes. I will sleep on the streets, sharing their hunger.'

She turned right towards Golden Wheat Street and strode spiritedly towards the house where she was born. She was told it was her father himself, an experienced nurse, who pulled her soft head towards him, then lifted her upwards, grinning from ear to ear, shortly before the ambulance arrived.

She did not know much about her father apart from the numerous photos which had hung in the living room since he died in a car accident. They were removed when her mother remarried, except one photo featuring him sitting next to her mother, with Ruth in his lap.

To the right in the photograph Fiona is seen standing, giving a shy smile to the photographer, placing her hand on her father's shoulder. The photograph has remained a testament to a transient family happiness. The new husband tolerates it gracefully. Alongside it he put a larger photograph of himself, indicating his silent existence.

Ruth did not wish her mother or stepfather to come out of the house until she had passed by in peace. She did not want her mood spoilt. Her heart raced while she watched the house from the opposite pavement. The front was as it used to be, the small front garden, the wooden gate which she'd opened and closed on many occasions. She remembered sitting on the door steps, her skinny legs covered with the playful scratches of childhood. Sitting with her doll. And the two windows, overlooking the street, their lower half hidden by the acacia trees. She wondered why she had come back to this place, which looked as though she had left it many centuries ago. Although it was only four years later, the two episodes in her life were separated by an epoch.

Why did she not get along with her stepfather? Fiona got along very well with him. She called him 'Uncle Paul'. But Ruth loathed him. She would often sit at her mother's side and steal a look at him, always remaining a stranger. She would always remain quiet whenever he was around. She would avoid him, as a deer would a hunter. When she became a little older she began to withdraw from her mother, as they would often argue. She became more and more withdrawn. She would go out to play for longer. Everyone was preoccupied with themselves, including Fiona. Ruth became reckless, unaware of her rash and often dangerous behaviour.

The first big argument was when she defended herself against every one. It was the day she dropped out of school.

She had stayed away from home. She felt at peace with herself. She watched the trees, planted on both sides. They were cherry trees and Panama berries. She recalled the long stick she used to hit the branches and make the cherries fall. Then she and Gina would pick up the fallen cherries, wipe them with their hands and put them in their mouths. Jennifer would bring a container, put it on the pavement then throw stones at the higher branches. Afterwards, they devoured the ripe and the half-ripe cherries. They continued to the end of the street, moving from one pavement to the other. People walked by without paying them any attention. Later they moved back, going up the street, stopping at some of the trees, their eyes hunting for the red cherries. Finally they turned back with Jennifer's container to share out the two or three cherries, lying at the bottom, among themselves.

Soon, the cherry trees appeared before her eyes and the Panama berries that flanked the street were growing bigger and becoming denser.

When she turned into Abundant Harvest Street she felt liberated from her memories, from the reminder of home, the mother, the husband and all that. She dashed blithely forward, oblivious to the pervasive smell that surrounded her, and to the people who passed by her and those she passed by, smiling at those she left behind. She returned to pondering her next refuge of choice, India.

She was a free spirit, wandering aimlessly in the universe. She neither expected people to make her happy nor wished to please anyone. When she secured the money, she would not return to the big jungle, London. She would never rejoin the marginalised who gave nothing back. Rather, they picked up the seeds in public squares, like city pigeons, which seemed to have lost the will to fly and learnt how to avoid car wheels instead.

She shall go to India. She visualised herself being adorned with necklaces of lilies by the locals, covering her all over with dyes and pink, yellow, and green powders, transforming her into a naked, blonde, Indian goddess. Passers-by would raise their joined hands in front of their faces and bow to her.

She sat with her legs twisted over each other, like the Indians in worship of her strange appearance—a naked body wearing nothing but an adornment of flower necklaces, and a mass of long, blonde hair hanging down her shoulders. With hands joined at the wrist, she smiled at the passers-by.

A blonde goddess had miraculously been born in India, a goddess with different features.

She sensed that she was climbing and that the streets were becoming narrower. Trees were rarer on route to Nancy's house. Her mind was jam-packed with thoughts and exciting images.

Unlike in the cities of England and the rest of the world, the roads of Three Hills tended to become narrower and the houses more concentrated on the outskirts, while being widely spaced in the centre. Prosperity prevailed in Three Hills around its centre.

Geographically, Three Hills like a fishing net, was replete with fish, stretching tightly upwards, becoming too narrow, its rhombuses totally disappearing and expanding downwards. The earliest buyers in Three Hills, who paid a high premium, were fortunate to own a property on wide streets, around Sticky Trap Street; whereas the late buyers who paid less got smaller houses, built on narrow streets reminiscent of the remaining old alleys seen in the centres of London, Rome and Beijing. These met the needs of pedestrians, but when any cart pulled by a single horse came along, the driver would call out to pedestrians to mind out!

These are but financial schemes. They do not care much about modern planning, and certainly of no concern to Ruth anyway.

Ruth stood outside one of the doors and pressed the doorbell. After a while, the door opened slightly and a woman in her forties emerged and recoiled as she recognised Ruth. She demanded, 'Ruth! What do you want?'

'I've come to see Nancy!' She smiled at the woman. 'Is she home?'

The woman hesitated initially then said, decisively, 'No, she's not.'

Meanwhile, Nancy appeared in short trousers. On seeing Ruth she said, in a mixture of astonishment and pleasure, 'Ruth!' She stepped outside to hold Ruth by the hand. 'You are in Three Hills!'

'Yes,' replied Ruth meeting her friend's smile with a wider grin.

Everything happened so swiftly that the woman, Nancy's mother, was taken by surprise. She looked embarrassed, but soon regained her resolution. She called out at Nancy, 'You're not allowed to go into the street in those clothes!'

Nancy ignored her mother's warning. 'You look gorgeous!' she said.

'You too!' Ruth returned the compliment.

'Are you staying in Three Hills? Tell me quickly,' asked Nancy.

'For a few days.'

'We are in for more trouble!' the mother remarked, almost as if she was talking to herself.

Nancy was twenty, plump, pretty, a little bit shorter than Ruth, and dim witted. She used to accompany Ruth from school. They would walk through the meadows on the Third Hill, which began where the houses ended, walking around the sheep, looking like a young, human flock. Then they would go down to the heart of town, wandering around the stores and the clothes shops, looking at the displays, conferring with each other about the merchandise displayed in the shop windows, then choosing the most expensive article in every shop, purchasing it in their fantasy world; fantasising about measuring it and wearing it. Afterwards they returned, loaded with delusions of being in possession of the prettiest dresses, hats and jewellery. Mrs Lander would ask in a furious voice, 'Where have you been? It's been three hours since school was over!' Without uttering a word, Nancy slipped inside, with Mrs Lander crying out behind her, 'Have you been with Ruth?'

Ruth, now standing next to her and smiling, went with Nancy once, carrying their swimsuits, to the nearest meadow, lying down on the grass, sunbathing. When a boy saw them, he fetched the rest of his friends. They gathered together, watching and making comments, winking at one another about the naked exposure on the farm. Rumours circulated in Three Hills that Ruth and Nancy had taken off their tops to reveal their breasts to soak up the summer heat.

Others even claimed that the lower pieces were removed to let the sun scorch their rears. Three Hills residents' imaginations ran wild, adding more varied scenarios. Since that day, Nancy had been detained at home. Her freedom to go out was severely curtailed. She was prevented from meeting up with Ruth.

When Ruth offered to go with her to the town centre, Nancy said to her mother, 'Mum! I'm going with Ruth to the coffee house.'

'You're not going anywhere' said Mrs Lander resolutely, stepping down and grabbing her daughter's hand.

Nancy pulled her hand back with less severity, speaking in a plaintive voice with some embarrassment, 'But I'm only going for half an hour, Mum, please!'

'We have had enough already as it is,' the mother pronounced, trying to grab Nancy's arm. 'You are not going in this piece of clothing.'

'Please, Mum, I will be wearing a long dress.' She reached with her free hand for Ruth's hand. Ruth was astonished at what was happening.

'I said you're not going anywhere,' firmly reiterated the mother. 'Get inside the house, now!'

'Please!' Nancy tried to avoid her mother, appealing for Ruth's help. 'Ruth, tell her, please.'

Ruth intervened when she realised that Nancy was a virtual prisoner in her own home. 'You can't stop her from going out! She's twenty years old!'

'Please,' said Mrs Lander firmly, 'it's not your business. You'd better leave now.'

The mother held Nancy, clinging to her with both hands, pulling her towards the door, while the girl pleaded, her resistance weakening. Her pleas became less vehement, and ultimately she gave in to her mother's authority.

'Cow!' Ruth shouted at the top of her voice.

'Thank you!' responded Mrs Lander indignantly. 'What would one expect from a girl like you?' She slammed the door shut.

Ruth had had deep-rooted sympathy for Nancy since the days of their youth, turning into a form of superficial affection, ingrained in her troubled emotions. Nancy's dimwittedness had rendered her endearing to Ruth, especially as Nancy used to reveal to Ruth what was happening at Nancy's home, and her own suppressed desires, most of which were naive or bizarre. This created in Ruth a weird, motherly feeling. Mrs Lander's behaviour seemed totally unfair and unacceptable to her.

She tightened her lips in resentment and murmured some words under her breath. Finally she spoke aloud to herself. 'The cow!'

Her mother used to sit opposite Nancy at the window so that she could keep an eye on the road, so that her lover might sneak unnoticed in through the back garden gate. What right did she have to impose her overprotection upon Nancy?

Ruth had once not cared for family or relatives, close or distant. She had long turned her back to the wind, which blew her away in whatever direction. However, she once heard the teacher mention something about hereditary genes, and this had been firmly imprinted in her mind. It had never gone away. It kept returning in her memory. It cropped up in her mind every time she rebelled against prevailing customs. She was copying what she had inherited from her family and was not responsible for her foolish behaviour. Although her mother was known for her temperance and, according to what she had heard, her father had never behaved foolishly, her own folly was buried deep inside that coded, helical, twisted structure.

Ruth walked down through narrow roads, which the

council had long neglected to repair, in the direction of the town centre, passing boys and children using the pavements and the roads as a playground. She looked at them with a mixture of emotions: love, apprehension and fear. She quickly dismissed the mix, turning her face to keep it out of her way. Instead, her fantasy summoned the image of the naked blonde goddess, surrounded by the Indian worshippers, feeling the faint, tingling sensation spiralling up through her legs into her shoulders, spreading through her body and finally resting in her heart.

Sticky Trap Street used to be quite busy with shoppers, revellers, celebrating the weekend, the aimless loiterers that typified the town centre. The remaining rain water, mixed with sewage water, ran down through the narrow streets and higher-up lanes to settle finally in the centre, forming a lake through which people waded in their long wellingtons boots, moving among the stores, the coffee houses and the bars, whose doors were barricaded with sand bags. Some were irritated. Others were joking about the chaos that had befallen Three Hills.

No one listened to individual complaints, and no one cared about the collective objections. The breakdown in services had become the butt of jokes for some, but others responded with muted fury. Meanwhile, an atmosphere of joyous celebration prevailed among the young men and women. The young women were dancing, hopping in the water and singing. The boys joined in, oblivious to the cause of the merriment that had taken hold of them. The grownups and the elderly smiled at this public manifestation of happiness, and everyone could discern the punishment inflicted on Three Hills. It had reached an unimaginable level, or so they reckoned, that what was happening was tantamount to recognition of their entitlement to the ten thousand pounds which slipped out of the computer inadvertently. Thus, the two sides had broken even.

Away from the joy which was visible on many faces, Mr Foreman and his wife sat in front of their cold, English breakfast, dejected, pondering the crisis that had befallen them and shaken up their daily routine.

At night, the water had moved suddenly and rapidly across the low doorsteps, spreading out its slithering tongue underneath the doors to fill up the kitchen, the halls, the bedrooms and the bathroom, stretching out further into the small living room, creating along its way a formation of linked lakes, filling at the rate of half a centimetre an hour.

Mrs Foreman had been into her second dream. She found herself making tea for three female guests sitting at the kitchen table. She filled the teapot with water and, once it became empty, would refill it, repeating the process. Mr Foreman, now out of his second dream and into the third, found himself in a sailing boat, rapidly racing the wind, pulling behind it some graceful, black horses, sparks flying under their hoofs while they galloped across the surface of the sea, pulling a carriage loaded with straw. When the water reached their bed and the drench seeped through their pyjamas, they woke up simultaneously by a cold sting. Their hands now were touching the surface of the bed, and feeling around the brimful soak-age. They stared at each other in disbelief, each posing a mental question, 'Did you wet the bed?'

The English breakfast remained untouched, in front of them. The coffee had gone cold, untouched. They had lost their appetites. Their minds and thoughts were miles away in the small, elegant house which was ruined by the waters. They now compared their customary, daily breakfast in the family kitchen with this oily, soggy, greasy breakfast lying, in defiance, on the table. Each from their own perspective ran away, back in time, to the day they were led, blindfolded, into their disheartening fate, in search of peace and tranquillity in Three Hills, where they hoped to spend the rest of their life.

Mr Foreman said, 'At the end of the day, we have wasted away our life's dream.'

'Oh, yes...' said Mrs Foreman.

'And we have swapped it for a water-logged pit in Three Hills,' Mr Foreman went on to say.

'Oh yes, a hole where everything we have saved up

has sunk!' echoed Mrs Foreman.

'Paper! All our dreams have been nothing but paper,' affirmed Mr Foreman.

'Oh, paper turned into a soggy mush, no more, no less,' replied Mrs Foreman.

'If you had listened to me we would not have chosen this hole!' continued Mr Foreman.

'Oh, yes?' she challenged. 'It was you who was enthusiastic about this choice.'

'If you had said "No" I would not have bought this house!' said Mr Foreman.

'But I didn't say "Yes", did I?' asked Mrs Foreman.

'And did you say "No" clearly enough?' he inquired.

'How could a "No or a "Yes" be clear enough if luck is so opaque and unpredictable?' asked Mrs Foreman.

'We were concerned about the future!' asserted Mr Foreman.

'Oh yes,' said Mrs Foreman, then added, 'that one, itself, was unpredictable, so long as it was under the protection of the establishment!' said Mrs. Foreman.

'We were misled by the publicity!' said Mr Foreman.

'We often are easily swayed by publicity, and after a while we regret it,' concurred Mrs Foreman.

'I was, in fact, hesitant,' continued Mr Foreman.

'I was hesitant, too,' said Mrs Foreman.

'You didn't explain your hesitance,' said Mr Foreman.

'I was respecting your feelings.'

'But I was in a dilemma regarding the existence of several parks!'

'You miss the point. The word "several" does not specifically mean anything!'

'But it does not mean nothing at all. The problem lies in the language they use, which gets you nowhere. It appeals to unstable aspirations,' Mr Foreman went on in a tone that concealed his blame.

'I thought a single public park near the house would suffice!'

'These are what I call the shaky aspirations that prevent one from scrutinizing the content of the advertisement!'

'I had left it for you to read thoroughly.'

'They conceal their deception in the final and small paragraph. That's why I told you to give it more of your attention!' shot back Mr Foreman, attempting to lay the blame on his wife.

'And the rivers! They said there were two rivers in Three Hills!'

'Repugnant!' said Mr Foreman, suppressing his rage.

'Much more could be said, yet nothing can be changed!'

'We used to be happy in our old house,' said Mr Foreman.

'Ambition, at an age like ours, was bound to invite trouble!' conceded Mrs Foreman. 'We spent all we had managed to save on top of the proceeds from selling the house! At least we will be compensated by the insurance,' she remembered, somewhat triumphant.

'The insurance! What do you think they are going to pay? Five per cent of the value of the house?' retorted Mr Foreman.

'At least we can have the water pumped out, have the walls repaired and re-painted.'

'That alone will require twenty thousand pounds, not forgetting the damage to the furniture!'

'And the clothes in the lower drawers, all soaked. They are of no use even to charity shops…'

'Certainly!' He shook his head in distress.

'And the kitchen utensils! They have to be replaced. You don't expect me to use articles contaminated by sewer water, do you?'

'We shall be forced to continue paying off our debts till the last day of our life.'

'You will pass away, and I will be the one burdened with the debts.'

'Who says?'

'I am five years younger than you are, have you forgotten!'

'Women often die before their husbands.'

'That was in the past. They used to tolerate unpleasant worries more than their husbands.'

Throughout this quiet pelting exercise, which could hardly be heard by anyone, the couple continued to lay the blame on each other.

When Ruth looked down Sticky Trap Street and saw the people engrossed in jubilation, each dancing to their own tune, shouting their heads off, she waded into the water like everyone else. She jumped and shrieked, kicking the water with her feet. She added more noise to the uproar, which reflected the reckless chaos boiling inside her.

India was back, sketching beautiful images in Ruth's mind. She visualised herself amongst a vast crowd of humans, half naked. Their bones protruding out of their skinny bodies. So she joined in with the gaiety of the revellers without giving it a second thought.

Her cheerful expression masked the anger she felt at the unacceptable behaviour of Nancy's mother, Mrs Lander. Therefore she burst forth, kicking at the water, spraying the crowd with it, laughing, whipping it with the front of her shoe towards whoever was near and whoever was far away. The laughter encouraged a group of teenagers to copy her water kicking. The fever caught on among the youths, and later the whole crowd joined in the fun. The water sprayed up to their necks, drowning them in the joviality and tumultuous chaos.

Ruth was overwhelmed by the general mirth. Her gleeful shrieks were louder than anybody else's. She became the centre of the tumult with the others revolving around her. She ran from end to end, then to the middle of the street. She was the focal point of laughter, shouting and spraying. At first she was the only girl in the jumble. Then a second girl entered the arena, followed by a third. Finally she was joined by a group of young girls, driven by the atmosphere. The two sexes joined hands in the early-morning, boisterous festivity.

Ruth exulted as she shrieked, moving her body and limbs vigorously. Her cries, against Fiona, Nick and Mrs Lander, and other people who took issue with her and were judgemental about her behaviour, grew louder. She wanted to find out the reason for the pleasure. She leant towards an excited young man standing next to her and shouted, 'Why is the street flooded with water?'

'Ruth!' At that very moment a voice came from behind.

'The sewage water doesn't go away,' replied the young man.

'Ruth!' The call became louder and a young man laid a hand on her shoulder. She looked behind.

'Ruth! Do you recognise me?' the young man asked, clinging to her.

'Who?' she asked.

'Chris,' came the reply, waiting for a response.

She stared at him, then said 'No!' and turned to resume the fun.

An old Toyota descended through a narrow lane

sloping down from the pastures in the gaping chasm between the first and the third hill, which the German Air Force believed the English warplanes used during investigative flights. It sped down Justice Street, skidding for a moment at the junction of Fragrance Street, then descended, shaking and rumbling around the potholes, breaking through the floodwater, then turning vigorously at the junction of Jubilations Street, its wheels screeching. It straightened up then accelerated, turning into Abundance Street. From there it joined Sticky Trap Street and continued shaking among the potholes. It finally came to a halt in the centre of the street before the Corporal Helmut and Co. Bar.

The driver, Mr Bob Dodge, stepped from the car and called out, 'Oh, Three Hills residents, I have discovered the secret!' Bob Dodge repeated his call in a louder voice.

The uproar subsided. A number of people now gathered around him, waiting with bewildered eyes for the secret he was going to share with them.

'I've just come down from the crevice between the first and third hills, and I noticed that the water pump was not working. The council has stopped the upper motor in order for the sewage water to fill the houses and streets of Three Hills. I saw that myself!'

The crowd looked up in the direction of the crevice. They mumbled with each other, then looked in disgust at the sewage water on the street.

Meanwhile, Bob Dodge was outraged, his jugular veins blown up. 'Half of this water you are wading in is dirt and grime discharged by the sewers.' He repeated, 'The motor that sucks the water isn't working. I've just come down from there. These are the doings of the council. Go up there and see for yourself!'

Revulsion and muttering pervade the mood of the crowd. The assembled people debated with each other on Sticky Trap Street, expressing various views. Bob Dodge and his Toyota shook with rage. However, in the end, when the ten thousand pounds vibrated in their memory, they all acknowledged, 'If it is the council we'll never be able do anything about it!'

The humming persisted among the gathering crowd and spread like wild fire, ultimately reaching the table at which Mr and Mrs Foreman were sitting in the Corporal Helmut and Co. Bar. It burst and landed there, extinguished.

Mr Foreman said to his wife, 'If the sewers are the source of the flooding, the insurance company will not pay a penny!'

The crowd began to disperse, each going his own way. Some went to coffee shops, others to bars for a drink or lunch. Ruth was walking by herself when she was approached by Chris, who was tailing her. He said, 'Ruth!'

Ruth turned around and was surprised to see him behind her. 'Ah, it's you again?'

'How about a cup of tea?' Chris asked.

'Okay…' Ruth replied nonchalantly.

They waded in the water until they reached the Corporal Helmut and Co. Bar. At the counter Chris asked, 'Half a pint of beer? If you wish?'

'You offered to buy me tea, not beer. You're desperate to take me to bed!' She let out a guffaw.

Chris smiled, his cheeks reddening with embarrassment. He then ordered two cups of tea. They carried them to a corner where they sat next to the table which Mr and Mrs Foreman had just left, leaving behind their untouched, cold English breakfast.

Gradually, Chris's countenance began to take shape in her memory, though indiscernible, obscure, like the many males who knew her, she thought, from school, or on account of her reputation as a reckless female, the talk of the town. But Chris, who was three or four years older than her, knew her very well and when he had spotted her among the crowd, kicking and shrieking, he followed her from a distance, then waded in the water, calling out her name, running through the crowd to lay his hand on her shoulder for fear of losing her again, as was the case seven years ago.

Now, there she finally was, sitting in front of him, a mature woman, somehow placid, cheerful, smiling and laughing, without a care in the world, but stinging in her responses as ever, still an adolescent at heart.

'I haven't seen you for such a long time in Three Hills!' said Chris, trying to break the silence that prevailed between them.

'I was in London,' she replied.

'That's why then! Did you find work there?' asked Chris.

'I spent my time loitering.' She smiled and responded sarcastically.

'The whole time?' asked Chris.

'What do you think people do there?' she asked. Chris shrugged. 'Look, I've made up my mind to go to India!'

'India! That's a good idea. Tourism?' Chris inquired.

'You could say that, but I intend to be an Indian goddess in the long run,' Ruth replied, adding milk to her tea, sipping some, while Chris stirred his tea bag in the cup so that the water might absorb its infusion.

He looked at her in disbelief. 'Then, will you find employment there?'

'Employment without taxes,' she replied with a hearty laugh.

'Why not!' Chris smiled in appeasement. 'As for me, I've been to fourteen job interviews and have not been successful in getting an offer!'

'You're a man of interviews!' she said sarcastically. 'You could create an interviewees club and the government would pay your salaries.'

'Good idea!' Joining in her satire, he added, 'And the State will deduct taxes from them!'

She laughed gleefully. 'You are dumb, like sheep!'

He laughed. 'What can we do? They call it "The Infernal Course of the Economy".' Then he added, 'Unless you find me work in India. A guard in one of your temples. Will you do that?'

'Maybe!' replied Ruth, smiling.

'You know my address, the abandoned clothes factory. Do you remember, it?'

'Oh, you are Chris who...' and she remembered.

'Yes, you do remember it, don't you?' He drew her into the recollection, looking into her eyes sparkling in astonishment.

She smiled, resting her chin on her hand. 'I hardly recognised you because of... your hair. It must have peeled off rapidly!'

Smiling, he moved his hand over the front of his bald head, as if inspecting it. 'It is like fate, lurking around to catch the young before reaching adulthood. In fifty years' time, babies will be born without hair on their heads.'

She had been seventeen when Chris lured her into the abandoned clothes factory. After they passed the pastures, they went down the other side of the third hill and into a tall building capable of accommodating a hundred male and female workers. In the past it had been buzzing with activity. Fabric used to be woven there, waterproof clothes sewn—coats, shirts, protective head gear—to guard against the rain for which England became renowned in the sixties of the last century. Then the factory fell victim to the recession because of soaring prices and tax increases. The factory owner sold the franchise to a Hungarian company, which later began exporting the same ready-made clothes to England at lower prices.

Among dust-coated, abandoned machines and cold sewing tables, Chris chatted her up then deflowered her. She went home happy with her first full sexual experience.

Ruth remembered the place, with its rusted roof and machines enshrouded in dust. She remembered that she used to seek refuge there after running from the torturous arguments with her mother. The longer she stayed there, the longer it would worry her mother. Or so she hoped. The place became a shelter for foxes and their young. Huge rats scurried about and leapt at her while she cringed in terror. She couldn't sleep a wink.

'Shall we go up there one more time?' Chris asked, adding in a low, conspiratorial voice, 'I have a condom.'

'You always keep one in your pocket!' she replied, laughing, then smiling. 'No condom. I'm no longer afraid. I've had my uterus removed.'

'Oh, my God!' He was stunned. 'At your age?'

'Yes,' she replied. After a short silence she added, 'I am no longer interested in making love.'

Chapter 4

The council chairman, Liam Hudson, stood on a small coffee table, reading from a sheet of paper, bringing it closer to his eyes for a while, then holding it away from them a moment later. He then delivered a speech.

'Ladies and gentlemen, you may, no doubt, be wondering why I am looking forward to your support in this political post. I say to you that England desperately needs to rise rapidly; therefore, it requires loyal, competent men who are primarily loyal...'

Rose Bennet, the secretary, opened the door and entered. She walked towards the council chairman, lifted her eyes to him and said, 'Your voice is excessively loud. You will have to keep it down a little bit to let it have the desired effect on the audience. And why are you standing on the table?'

'I suppose if I stand on a raised platform, I will be able to capture the attention of everyone in the rally; unless you have a better proposal?' implored Mr Hudson expectantly.

'You would have to stand on the bureau so that people can see your shoes as well. You also forgot to mention the word "committed", which is profoundly resonant!' The secretary held a second copy of the speech, studying the full impact of his words on the audience from near and far, even from behind doors.

'Primarily committed and loyal... Like so!' He observed the effect of the words on the secretary.

'That's much better,' she replied, approvingly.

Mr Hudson stepped down from the table with the written speech in his hand, looking unhappy about something. He lapsed into a pensive mood for a while. Then he said, 'It would seem that these words are overused, repeated by all politicians. It would be a good idea to follow Mr Gallow's advice, to use suggestive words, symbols. We ought to be unique, to be able to offer something new, something unprecedented!'

'What does this word you have just mentioned mean, if you don't mind?' asked the secretary.

'Suggestion!'

'Seduction?!' she repeated after him.

'Meaning, to refer to things indirectly, without naming them.' He threw the sheet of paper on the bureau. 'We create a new language, a style of address beyond what people are familiar with.' His thoughts racedfurther through his mind. 'We have to make our audience singularly prone to misunderstand what we specifically say, so that they may understand only in the End.' His flight of fancy took him even further. 'It is a new language, emerging from the bottom of the heart, flowing straight into the heart of the audience.

Are you with me?'

'Certainly, Mr Hudson,' replied the secretary, who was sitting on the settee, absent-minded, pondering her long-suffering heart. Her skirt was slightly pulled upwards to reveal her seductive thighs.

Mr Hudson tried several resounding expressions without being able to capture one that would give the finishing touches to the heart-felt proposed new terms ___ his new style of address. He sought to delude people by opening their eyes and ears to his carefully formed words, which meant everything, yet signified nothing. His imagination played out images of the attendees wildly applauding him, extolling the virtues of his experimental method of handling England's crisis, which no one had given much consideration or care to.

His feverish fantasy soared up in his smoky head. Imaginary coverage from local newspapers played out in front of him, displaying his photograph across the front pages. This was later echoed by the international newspapers, all hailing the emergence of a pioneering, model policy, such as England had never experienced since Disraeli. England was back to its former glory, back to the creativity of its Renaissance.

As for Rose, she let her imagination race after her melancholic mood, closely following Mr Hudson's movements and studying his hand gestures, without hearing what he was saying. She imagined him as a

Greek statue, harmoniously co-ordinated, but otherwise cold.

She wondered why there was a sudden relapse in her burning passion, and early widowhood in her infatuation. Could it be a spell of envy, cast by the other council secretaries? Or could it be the smoke that incessantly circled his head in waves? Or was it the vengeful desire of his wife to retain him all for herself, even though he was reduced to a torso without a phallus! Relapse

'Yes!' said Rose. 'Yes!' was repeated like the returning echo inside the cave of her murky soul.

It was nine in the evening. The employees had gone home. Silence prevailed within the council's walls. However, his wife had not called in to find out why he was delayed at the office. She was not fretting over his return home, or whether or not he was coming back.

In the past, when his sex organ was alive and kicking, eyeing women up left and right like a meerkat, her telephone had never stopped ringing, reverberating in her head like an electric drill, *din... din....* A lifeless corpse had now been delivered to Rose.

'He is busy now.' Rose's words sank deeper into her inner self. At times she would murmur the words inaudibly, barely escaping her lips. 'He is, no doubt, exhausting himself in an attempt to choose the right words, to get his first public speech ready. All his senses are focused on what might please the people; he does not think of my happiness. He is neglecting his health; he does not think of a cure to his problem. He attempts, instead, to find solutions for the ills of England. Where would I, a drop, be in this deep ocean?'

Her mind was whirling. 'It was Mr Gallow who got him into politics, whispering in his ears that he would be able to bag money, glory and women! But... will he, with a rag dangling between his legs, be able to sweep women off their feet?'

In the end, whatever the consequences, Rose made up her mind to cling on to him obstinately. She was convinced, prompted by her naive, feminine instinct, that Mr Hudson was hers alone. She would shield him from desperate women and continue to feed his body with her gypsy, magic formula—through percolating herbal extracts disguised within the coffee, tea and water he drank—until she had cured him of his sexual indisposition. Soon his penis would rise, healthy, standing tall, at full sail. Her body would entwine with his, like an ivy plant, inhaling his rancid smell one more time and for last, dying in the pelvis of his two florid legs.

But who is this Gallow? And why, all of a sudden, has he materialized in the midst of her calamity? And why does he want to wrench his attention to politics?

George was a lowly journalist. He worked as a

correspondent for the Capital newspapers, reporting from the Midlands, and was later sacked for news fabrication. Afterwards, he went down to London where he was employed by one of the tabloid papers. But he was sacked soon after it was discovered that he was hyping up reports. He remained unemployed but kept close to the fledgling political media and the young and ambitious, lying in wait for the opportunity to climb the professional ladder.

During one of his visits to London, the council chairman met Mr Gallow by chance. Later they drank whisky until their eyes popped out. Mr Hudson found in Mr Gallow's conversations and philosophy an outstanding grasp of the school of opportunism, which caught his attention; whereas Mr Gallow found that he had hit upon a raw specimen, a robber in his own narrow field, worthy of mentoring and careful nurturing!

Gallow was convinced that politics was the quickest route to riches. And because he was of middle-class background, he ploughed his arduous way across journalism, trudging along its margin and remaining middle class at heart. He catapulted himself into the political milieu and acted like a man of creed. He argued, participated in discussion with politicians and their aides, and made proposals, until he finally stumbled into Liam Hudson, who revealed to him the financial deals which he had undertaken.

Gallow believed that what Hudson called 'hits' were but trivialities in his own narrow field.

Despite the council chairman's boldness and his impetuous audacity in striking deals and imposing profit percentages on companies, the practice remained inadequate, and limited to the sphere of a county comprising only five towns of varying size. Whereas in politics, nationally, deals would cover vast sections with sizeable budgets large enough to make your head spin.

Council management required caution and hesitation, but in politics there were trickery and games, played in the dark, and numerous enough for one to hide behind employees, lower in rank. The situation also led to a multitude of responsibilities and diversity, which made the entangled and complicated line disappear before reaching the Big Head!

Perhaps it was British policy, according to Gallow's speeches, which allowed, through fatigue, the proliferation of huge knots on the ropes it often threw to politicians, so that they might turn somersaults without fear of tumbling.

'This is not indolence, Mr Hudson,' whispered Mr Gallow in the council chairman's ear, throwing his arm flatteringly around Mr Hudson's back, 'but a ruse in order for England to entice the middle class, our class, to politics and keep the aristocrats away! Do you see what I mean? The age of integrity has gone forever.'

Mr Gallow adjusted his posture and adopted the appearance of a well-informed person. 'Because it is unfair and hinders the State's performance, making it unbearably boring and dull. The regulations need to be dismantled. The network of responsibilities ought to be widened and crammed with middlemen. It is this measure that will stimulate the economy and the performance of the government, and ensure that smiles return to all faces!

'Frankly,' Mr Gallow went on, in order to finish his conversation with Hudson, 'this is the age of billionaires. Nowadays people talk about fifty or a hundred million only in jest! Fifty billion, yes! But talking about millions is ridiculous, believe me! There are five undisclosed cities in England where people clandestinely deposit funds and are exempted from paying tax. The government is fully aware, yet acts as if it were in the dark. All this to favour few individuals and allow them to wallow in wealth!'

The council chairman remembered his conversation with Gallow, recalling it as he would the commandments, going in pursuit of the words of advice and prediction uttered by Gallow at that soiree.

Finally, he came out of his daydream with a start. He returned to the office, the secretary, and the paper which he was still holding.

'It appears that Mr Gallow alone is able to draft this speech!' he said addressing his secretary, 'I cannot find a word that says what it does not signify! This calls for an experienced specialist. Anyway, it is not the council chairman's business, is it?'

Rose stood from her soft chair and wondered, 'And this speech?'

'Tear it up!' replied Mr Liam Hudson. He began tearing up the sheet of paper and pushing parts into the shredder. The secretary did the same with her copy.

'A little bit of whisky to calm down your tired nerves?' Rose asked, coming closer to Mr Hudson, tenderly wiping his sweaty forehead.

'No, thank you.' He sighed.

While he was getting ready to go out she put her hand on his lower thigh, massaging it, moving her hand upwards, stopping at the zip. It slid open. She sneaked her skilled fingers inside, mustering all her experience to exact arousal. She went on feeling him, studying his reactions after he had surrendered to her act of foreplay, pretending to adjust his necktie. However, her efforts and manual dexterity were met by a stubborn shrinkage.

She said loudly, closing the zip, 'Not yet?' Then, as she turned to go, she said to herself in a whisper, 'Not a single vein in it has swollen up!'

'I am meeting Gallow tomorrow,' he said, as if he were talking on a different planet.

-2-

On the following day, and before going to the appointment which he had arranged earlier with Gallow, the council chairman met with CEOs of what was called 'Road Surfacing and Maintenance'.

He was desperate to learn about their methods for fiddling inventories and creating secret deals. The meeting with them was vital, but so was the meeting with Gallow. He had decided during one of his sleepless nights to appoint Gallow as a political adviser, seeking his assistance in writing modern speeches, and his advice on electoral issues and designing election campaigns. Therefore he kept looking at his watch, lest he should miss the next meeting.

'Complaints made by citizens about potholes and indentations on the edges of the roads are increasing on a daily basis. And though we don't take these things seriously enough, the reports by the council's surveyors suggest that the pitch used to fill up the holes and repair the road often sticks to the wheels of the first car that passes over it, scattering it outwards. I've seen pictures taken with a mobile phone confirming that you dig up roads that are in good condition, then have them surfaced with asphalt. You get paid twice, once for digging and once more for repair. We shall set these reports aside as well.

However, I hear, and my hearing has never failed me, that you defraud the state and evade paying your taxes and council rates! What is your comment on that?'

The CEOs of the companies were astounded and aghast at the accusation. They turned to one another enquiringly. Many a sleeved arm—decorated with tattoos of snakes, graphic designs, naked girls, and eastern and western embellishments—with one voice denied the accusations.

The council chairman hushed them into silence and said, 'Google displays a map showing the cities and villages and the roads linking them that come under the council's administration. It pinpoints from space the asphalt-covered potholes like brightly lit spots close to each other, turning the region at night into a blazing torch. So how come your returns show overwhelming losses year in, year out?'

The vipers, the naked women, and the embellishments spoke back in protest and in wild denial, laying the blame on the hike in the price of fine sand, gravel, dust, asphalt, tar and petrol, and the costs of mechanical repairs. The uproar escalated while everyone simultaneously recounted the losses incurred in their work, claiming that they were hardly able to provide food for their wives and children.

The council chairman raised his hands once more, asking them to keep quiet as he was unable to hear their complaints clearly. He tapped his forefinger on the face of his watch, suddenly realizing time was flying by.

'Please stop the noise, will you? Will someone tell me the secret, the riddle implicitly agreed upon between yourselves? How do you make your annual records appear as having incurred losses, when I know you make millions of pounds out of the council using thin layers of asphalt that don't stand a chance in the face of a haphazard storm?'

Bewildered, they looked at each other, wondering what secret the chairman was talking about, what millions he was referring to. They had made it clear that they received the money from the council's accountant to distribute among the workers and the supply traders! So what secret was he alluding to, since they go to bed on half an empty stomach?

The fat arms piped down, lost for words, and so too the tattoos, permanently marked in big, brightly coloured lines. They turned their hands, twiddling their fingers, shocked at hearing such a serious accusation. They dismissed it as harsh, unfair, false and totally irrelevant, and insulting to their professional loyalty.

Meanwhile, the council chairman's forefinger nervously tapped his watch.

He looked into their bewildered eyes, which were probing into his, seeking the source of the new accusation, its origin, its roots, and how it singled them out.

'We, Mr Chairman, tolerate and withstand the losses for the glory of England!' one of them interjected. His comment was seconded by the other three, who praised his quick wittedness.

'Oh yes, certainly!' Mr Hudson replied sarcastically. Changing his tone, he said, 'The council, gentlemen, pays you twenty million pounds a year, so how come your returns come back laden with losses? I only want to know how your charts go below zero. I need to know the method you use to manipulate the figures!'

'Without doubt the chairman has lost his marbles!' the company bosses whispered among themselves and, once more, the naked women, the whales, and the decorations on eight fat arms, shifted uncomfortably, debating in a hushed voice the council chairman's direct and open request regarding alleged manipulation of documents and budget figures. The glory of England had temporarily shrunk with fear because the chairman wanted to know the secret! —

There was no secret to conceal; they had agreed among themselves, but it was their deep secret that big and small companies emulate, to ensure that the glory of England was safeguarded. It was business as usual, and the number of returns or losses would go to the tax office so as to determine the Gross Domestic Product, be it with closed eyes or negligence. So, what nonsense was the chairman talking about, nonsense about what he called the 'method of fiddling'?

The council chairman was running late for his second appointment, while the vipers and naked girls, gyrating in front of him, pronounced nothing of merit. The wrestling match between the watch's hands and their procrastination increased his tension. Meanwhile, his worried looks shifted between his left hand and the ruddy arms and faces flexing their muscles.

Having lost his patience and, to put an end to the questions and answers which were going off target, shortening the time he had set aside for the meeting with Gallow, he finally said to them, 'If you insist! You alone will be responsible, in that case, to the people for the maintenance. We will deny all responsibility for road maintenance. As from tomorrow, we will announce the council's willingness to pay, giving you the freedom to do the maintenance to your own standards!'

The faces turned to look at one another and whispered among themselves while Mr Hudson watched them from his office, his forefinger rapping the face of the watch with intensity. With one voice the faces finally said, 'As your Excellency wishes.'

They understood that they were no longer liable except for the issues contained in the letters of complaints. But who cares about complaints?

The council chairman knew half the secret, which

was that the four companies belonged to one person, sitting among them, pretending to be running his own company; and that the companies supplying the fine sand and coarse sand and the tar operated independently but, in the long run, were all answerable to him. The presumed losses would be distributed across small companies. They persisted in making losses yet, split up, the losses seemed too small to catch the eye of Big Brother!

As for the second half of the secret, relating to fiddling the figures, the council chairman would never be able to find out, even if four more chimneys sprang from the top of his head.

Despite all that, the complaints continued to arrive in their thousands, only to end up in jute sacks, unseen by anyone. The companies were unaware of their existence.

The men left, hiding their satisfaction with the outcome. Then Rose entered. Her eyes were red, encircled by insomnia-induced swelling. The council chairman, adjusting his appearance in a hurry, said, 'I'm going to see Gallow. No one should know I'm meeting up with him!' Then he left, shrouded in secrecy.

Hesitant and uncertain, Rose opened the windows for ventilation, ridding the stagnant air of the smoke and the bad breath. She put the scattered papers back together again on the surface of the bureau. She then inhaled and exhaled, letting out a big sigh over the vacuum left behind by the council chairman, before finally returning to her room.

-3-

It had been three months since November. Winter proved to be very chilly. There was absolutely no change.

At the end of January, when it started to snow heavily, the council chairman began to appreciate politics, and enjoyed preparing for election. He had already delivered four stylistically modern speeches that he did not comprehend, which nevertheless were received with enthusiasm by an audience hungry for whatever was new and different. Mr Hudson enjoyed the applause tremendously, and he returned home exhilarated and in high spirits, smiling at everyone he came across, effusively shaking hands with the well wishers. He would throw himself onto the bed and go to sleep immediately, dreams of success taking him higher in a flight of fantasy, overflowing with money, influence and women.

However, he did not forget about Three Hills and its dead silence over the ten million pounds, which had been forcibly withdrawn from his personal account. Despite that, his balance had trebled via the commissions he received from the companies, which sold their products in the region, and from the adopted austerity policies, making a great number of official workers and teachers redundant. But his greedy eyes remained firmly on Three Hills' residents, licking their skins with a coarse tongue, through the flesh and down to the bone.

Rose Bennet had spent the last two months driving her Volkswagen through the gypsy camps that sprawled across the towns of the Midlands, begging the old women and men to find a healing remedy for Mr Liam Hudson, whose sexual energies had waned while he was still in the prime of his second youth.

She did not entirely ignore the newer medications. She had given him tablets of Viagra and its derivatives with water. She even inserted her hand into the front opening of his trousers, feeling and examining the reluctant object. Still, she failed to receive any encouraging sign. She went back to arranging and listing the names of the recommended herbs, the ones already in use and those undergoing clinical trials, as well as the folded amulet, inscribed with unintelligible tongues invoking the jinn, the dead and the living. She marked them with dates and distinguishing features: TRIED, INEFFECTIVE and UNDERGOING TRIAL.

As for David and Fiona, there was no changeof circumstance. Nothing new had occurred to their small family.

David's absent-mindedness fluctuated between high

and low, and the same pattern was true of his hearing and sexual feelings. Fiona's scissors continued harvesting the hair of customers, dyeing it black, pale blonde or dark blonde, to mask its early or sweeping whiteness. She sought a method that would revitalize David in bed, but she seriously could not care less about the side effects of his comas.

And to devote herself to that grief which consumed a huge part of her thought, she gave her sister, Ruth, one thousand pounds in order to get her off her back. Ruth went back to London, with the tatty India book and its missing pages.

The only re-location done was by the retired Mr Foreman and his wife, as they moved out into a second-rate hotel situated at a distance of fifty metres away, opposite the council building. There, it appeared, they had begun their final life journey, their house having been badly damaged by the stagnant sewage and rain water that remained in the rooms. Its walls were covered with algae and rot. So the Foremans started making frequent visits to the council, demanding compensation.

The defence for the rights of the claimant and for those of the defendant were taken up by highly paid solicitors who were well versed in the law and its loopholes, governing complaints that were complicated yet simple at the same time. They manipulated the weaker details every time Mr and Mrs

Forman's complaint reached a conflict point between the two entitlements, a deliberate adjournment was proposed as a means of procrastination.

Despite all that, the Foremans persisted in carrying their papers and documents, every morning, in a bulging plastic bag, heading toward the council building, hoping to find a solution to the problem.

Although unwritten English laws that derive their legality from former cases and summations of former fair and flexible rulings, with the intention of scrutiny in some cases; however, with skilful and canny solicitors who have made a career of dragging the cases into a whirling vortex, it is ensured that not a single clear-cut line is discernible. Thus, it is transformed into a procrastination exercise, a labyrinth that becomes deadly frustrating to a deserving claimant.

In the case of the Foreman, their flooded home had been transmuted into a tug of war between the insurance company, saddled by problems brought about by the rain water, and the council, which was responsible for the behaviour and conduct of sewage water!

They took their breakfast and coffee nearly every day at the hotel. Afterwards, they left for the council, carrying their plastic bag bulging with documents and correspondence between the insurance company lawyers and the council. They stood in long queues, to be seen by officials who impatiently listened to each intricate complaint.

In this condition, the Foremans remain shrouded in grief, taken from the daily rituals they used to perform at their house, which is now destroyed and pervaded by the sewage water. Their small family was forced to pay for the hotel, lunch and dinner meals at cheap restaurants out of the ten thousand pounds, they had received, and what they had saved up for their old age. Thus life contrived its twisted justice. Time, meanwhile, had not ceased gnawing through their health, bringing on their end at an accelerated rate.

Mrs Foreman woke up earlier than her husband in the morning. She sat on the edge of the bed, her eyes hitting the wall, feeling its proximity, almost touching her nose. She moved her hand in front of her face for a while, until her eyesight adjusted to the true dimensions of the hotel room, whose walls were two metres wide and three and a half metres high. In addition to the narrow bed, there was a small commode, a mirror and a wardrobe. It contained a small bath, one metre in diameter, with a shower.

When Mrs Foreman wanted to go to the safe, Mr Foreman had to stand with his back to the bed to let her through. They had to do it alternately. The hotel room was so narrow they feel almost suffocated. Still, the hotel charged high rates, not simply because it faced the council building, but also because the criteria followed in its construction were laid in accordance with special engineering specifications.

In the hotel sector, and also in the construction of houses, markets, companies and government buildings, England followed rigid engineering planning, where rooms, corridors, electric lifts and windows tended to follow suit in a way that baffled the foreign visitor.

No one can determine the root causes of the latent feelings of depression that beleaguer the English person, and deprive him of the delight of spacious areas in construction. England has vast swathes of arable and waste lands, yet citizens confine themselves inside small houses, and construct installations and government buildings and supermarkets, huge from the outside but narrow on the inside, making maximum use of available space to the point that citizens have to walk with trepidation to avoid inconveniencing or imposing upon another.

Roads are built in cities or to connect them with one another. Car parks are constructed to take in cars, yet they are so narrow that traffic accidents occur, like scratching the car on contact with the walls, or minor accidents during the lengthy manoeuvres required to place the car in a rectangular slot with only centimetres to spare.

The Englishman, having attained civilized manners unrivalled in any other culture, compensates for being confined to a limited space with the much admired and equally envied ability to utter a quick apology for minor mistakes and mishaps, or for inadvertently encroaching upon someone's right of way while walking.

Is this feeling of depression down to the fact that the Englishman lives on an island, surrounded by water? Or is it that he watches the sedimentary coast, eastwards and westwards, being chipped away on a daily basis, with big chunks swept away by the waves, while governments are seemingly unperturbed by this worrying geological phenomenon? Or is it a legacy of the fathers and forefathers staying tightly next to one another, trying to keep warm in the cold weather, like a gaggle of penguins huddling together in the face of blizzards?

4

Mrs Foreman suffered from chronic pains in her legs, making it almost impossible for her to stand on her feet for more than a quarter of an hour.

Weeks after the house was flooded, and after her husband suffered a sudden illness, she had a blockage of the arteries in her thin legs and was immediately taken to hospital. There she was given four injections in each leg, to help open the blockage which was, according to the doctors, attributable to the unexpected psychological pressures. She was temporarily relieved of the pains that she felt when walking. However, the pain returned anew. On this occasion, she was given twelve injections, but the pain and discomfort eventually came back to stay with her. She felt them when she walked, or when she slept on her side for a long time at night.

In the middle of the night, when Mrs Foreman most needed to wrestle with and overcome her insomnia by intermittent dozes, the music would start from the building that adjoined the hotel at the back, subjecting her to the blaring trumpet and the thundering drum, so loud that it shook the narrow room, robbing her of the peace and quiet she craved in her struggle with the pain.

This raucous music is a new age by-product of the pandemonium culture. It copies or even competes with the "atomic" explosions that were designed for the ears. The electronic companies encourage their production and selling at high prices. And that is all that counts as far as they are concerned.

Mr Foreman, whose ears automatically shut down, slept soundly, dreaming, his cheek touching the pillow. His sleep flowed peacefully, uninterrupted throughout the night, as since his retirement ten years ago, he had been trying to compensate for the lost early spells of going to work very earl in the morning. However, the real reason for Mr. Foreman's profound slumber was a mechanism to rid himself of the nightly bouts of coughing which would return to him with vigour once he lifted his head off the pillow, due to the sudden heart attack he had sustained. This has coincided with the day his home was flooded, when they were thrown onto the middle of the road.

Mrs Foreman woke up in the morning after some anxious skirmishes, mostly not in her favour, with the noise coming from the building adjacent. The noise continued to the early hours of the morning. The sleepless night left puffed up eyes, drowsiness and unsteady steps. When moving inside the small room, she bumped into the wall once, and then into the bed, fumbling her way around under the faint light of the lamp on her way to the bathroom. She opened its door, pushing it inwards, revealing a narrow space, just enough to enable her to stand upright in front of the mirror and the sink, albeit hitting the back of the toilet seat. Armed with the instinct of a female, though failing to put it into perspective, she believes that the pains and the sleepless nights had sapped her face of its vitality and increased the depth of her wrinkles.

After washing her face with cold water, she sat on the edge of the bed, reminiscing about her well-kept kitchen and her daily kitchen rituals: preparing the family breakfast; standing for a while at the window overlooking a small, beautiful garden at the back; waiting for the water to boil so that she could pour it over the three tea bags in the teapot. The scented vapour rose to her nostrils. She placed the pot on the table that was covered with plates, butter, two jars of home-made apple jam, eggs, and toasted bread slices before her husband woke up.

She began thinking about her present daily life, crammed into a hanging cage on the third floor of the hotel. It had a small window, overlooking the corridor. Hot water was available only twice a week, due to the repairs that alternated between the pipes and the heaters. They loitered among the small restaurants to eat cheap meals through the noise of the trumpets and the rhythms of castanets and drums which interfered with her sleep. Her thoughts wondered back to her former life and the days of yore when it was so simple, quiet, with regular visits by neighbours, with the pervading chatter over tea and sweetened biscuits; or staying up late to watch comedies or repeats, or accompanying her husband, arm in arm, to the supermarket for their weekly shopping.

When her husband woke up, he coughed twice or three times and, with closed eyes, reached for the inhaler underneath the pillow, sucking deeply, filling his lungs with Phinolin. He asked, 'What day of the week is it today?'

'Wednesday,' replied his wife.

'Oh damn! Today is the council appointment! Have you forgotten?'

Waiting for their breakfast, the Foremans looked out the narrow window in the dining room. A fierce wind was blowing, shaking the glass. Snow had been falling since last night. They shivered with cold that penetrated the bones, despite the heavy clothes they were wearing. Feeling cold is primarily a sensation. If you stare cold in the eye from a relatively warm position, it will stare back at you with the same intensity, causing your body to shiver.

After the breakfast and morning coffee, the Foremans carried their papers and walked the fifty metres from the hotel to the council building, staying close to each other for warmth, weathering the strong wind that kept pushing them backward. On reaching the entrance, they shook the snow off their clothes and the swollen bag with its documents and letters of correspondence, exchanged between the solicitors representing the council and their counterpart, representing the insurance company, on the one hand, and between the two parties and themselves, on the other. Then, they joined the queue, awaiting their turn.

After half an hour, Mrs Foreman's leg pains flared up as a result of standing too long, trying to put up with it throughout, but now she was about to collapse when an employee offered her a chair next to her standing husband. Henceforth the chair hopped in time with the pace of the queue. Mr Foreman moved a few slow steps forward toward the official, his wife next to him, seated!

Mr Foreman pulled out the contents of the bag,

spreading out his letters and documents, arranging them chronologically on the counter, covering most of the surface area, leaving the rest in the bag, all dated and at the ready, to emerge on demand, reiterating on a daily basis the history and background of their case to the female official assigned to look into it.

Meanwhile, Mrs Foreman, seated, listened to the ongoing discussion, seeing neither the letters nor the female official.

At times she corrected dates misquoted by her husband, reminding him of events he had missed out and their chronology, while her husband was engrossed in elaborating on the case from A to Z, referring to the correspondence letters, the delays and the promises of reaching a solution and, finally, pointing to the time it had taken.

The wife had a fully functioning mental clock, too, and the lapse of two hours meant she needed to poke her husband, who was still busy talking, in the arm to alert him, ‘It is inhaler time.’

In response, he took the device from his pocket to take two doses of Phinolin to help open up his constricted tracheae, to be able to breathe in, in a semi-natural way, for a hundred and twenty minutes.

The female official remained seated behind the counter, signs of concentration on her face. She listened to the long, boring details of the case as told by Mr Foreman. However, her thoughts flitted now and again to the problem of her husband, who was addicted to gin, and to her sick daughter. She wondered whether he had given her her medication on time. She thought of the rancour among the employees and the inequality at work... Then she would give part of her attention to the current issue, already resolved in favour of the council and its famed solicitor.

But law and procedures demanded that she listened to everything the customers said. Then a single, brief note was added at the end: 'Summaries to be considered; claimants are to be informed about the outcome. The case is referred to another official for consideration.'

Foreman apologised for being too insistent, asking every male and female official why the case was referred yet again to officials he and his wife had already seen earlier. He explained to them, supporting his case with the documents spread out across the counter, only to receive the same reply and the very phrase: 'To be considered!'

'When will this consideration of the summaries happen, in order for this issue to be determined?'

Wishing to devote some of her time to thinking about her own, private affairs—at least for the ten minutes between this customer's departure and her calling out the name of the next customer—the female official explained politely, 'Procedural requirements.'

Ignorant of the procedures referred to, Foreman gathered together his letters and documents and tossed them back into the bag that was already bulging with paperwork. Mrs Foreman, stood up, ready to go. Her husband returned the chair to its place, expressing his gratitude to the official. They left the council building into the biting wind and the Midland snow.

Braving the wind and avoiding skidding, Mr Foreman debated with his wife the issue of going to a convenient coffee house or a pub, where they could eat a sandwich for dinner and spend two hours away from the cold. Mrs Foreman pleaded with him to remember her leg pains and select the nearest location instead of loitering in this dreadful weather.

Mr Foreman repeated that some of the places, especially the near ones, were absolutely suffocating and badly ventilated. Once inside his tracheae flared up, culminating in bitter bouts of coughing. Then there were the extortionate prices of coffee and tea!

Mrs Foreman agreed with his choice of convenience and muttered under her breath, 'Miserable he who doesn't own a house that gives him warmth and safety.'

She remembered their house, before moving out to Three Hills, where they had spacious rooms and windows that looked over the horse-chestnut tree, the oak and pine trees that spread out in orderly rows across a vast area of well-mowed lawn where, at dawn, birds could be heard joyfully warbling and chirping. Blackbirds hopped on the grass, busy, scurrying around in search of their meal of worms.

'Miserable he who doesn't own a house that gives him warmth and safety.'

Mr Foreman made room for his wife and she walked ahead of him into a small coffee house. He shook the snow from his clothes and took off his cap. They withdrew to a table away from the door, through which currents of cold air tumbled with every coming or leaving customer. He read the prices, looking for the cheapest sandwich with a hot cup of tea. Saving money stood vigilant in their minds, like a horrific devil staring down at them, questioning every pound they spent, while the ten thousand pounds slipped away through their fingers, spent on meals and hotel bills, even before a final decision that would determine their case was made.

After the waiter had toasted their bread slices, he filled up a teapot for two with boiling water and two teabags. He carried the lot with two empty cups and placed them in front of the Foremans. 'Enjoy your lunch!'

The couple ate their food, having lost their appetite. The husband missed out on the customary butter cube to spread out with the knife over the edges of the bread slice, because the cubes had run out at the coffee house and there was no one free to fetch some more from the supermarket.

Meanwhile, Mrs Foreman chewed her toasted bread with great deliberation, sipping her tea every now and again, reminiscing about her kitchen, well stocked with butter, jam and olive oil, which she used to pour over a plate of olives, in which to dunk small pieces of toast which she and her husband picked up with forks.

With their meal finished, the Foremans spent the remainder of the two hours exchanging blames over the haste with which they had sold their old house to move to Three Hills, having to use half of Mr Foreman's pension to pay off the loan, under the illusion of river views and public parks. Numerous exhausting and varied taxes burdened their income. Thus the happy days they had looked forward to in their old age were themselves, illusions.

Too many blames were exchanged in muted voices between them. They were like arrows going straight to the heart. Eventually they came to the realisation that they had been ensnared in an immoral trap set up by the banks and companies, causing them to fall into the grip of this merciless, wicked government establishment, the council!

The Foremans leaned against each other and walked towards the hotel, carrying some bread and thin slices of meat, along a road that had become slippery when it stopped snowing.

In summer, and after some improvement in the weather, the Foremans changed hotels three times, either in an attempt to escape the noise, or due to the narrowness of the room or the remoteness from the council. Some of the blood vessels in Mrs Foreman's legs became blocked and made it difficult for the blood to reach the heart, which led to paralysis of the lower parts of her body. This condition, in turn, intensified her pain and greatly shortened her intermittent spells of sleep at night.

The doctors advised the Foremans that she should stay at the hotel by day so that she did not become exhausted through having to walk. Her legs had been damaged by a great many injections and she could develop a serious blockage of the veins. However, Mrs Foreman insisted on accompanying her husband and sticking to him, as she had been doing for forty years. Were these doctors going to deprive her of being at his side when he would finally receive the compensation, specially as he often forgets some dates, appointments and the chronology of events? Who would remind him of all that?

November emerged once again. Snow started to fall, earlier than usual. Radio announcers and program presenters competed with one another at offering plausible explanations as to why such bizarre climatic phenomena which England had never witnessed the like of, for the last seventy years, should occur. They ascribed it to seriously big holes in the ozone layer. Others blamed the excessiveness in launching satellites which led to the formation of a dense cloud that hid part of the sun and diffused its heat energy.

The Foremans, however, did not seem to be swayed by these assertions and refused to be distracted by them.

Walking became a strenuous task for Mrs Foreman. Her husband began to feel the weight of her thin body on his left arm, while simultaneously holding the jute bag containing the documents and the letters of correspondence, which had, during the last months, doubled in size. It dangled by a string over his shoulder, and was held securely under his left arm.

Soon after the snow had stopped falling, the Foremans left the hotel and made for the council building, grappling with the blustering wind, walking cautiously on the pavement.

The Foremans eventually stopped in front a huge vehicle for loading used building materials and debris. They looked for a piece of wood, suitable for Mrs Foreman as a walking stick.

He selected a piece with nails still attached. 'This is the best throwaway piece for you to lean on!'

Mrs Foreman grabbed the piece of wood. It was heavy but would be reliable as a walking aid; at least it would enable her to avoid skidding.

Mr Foreman then added, as they walked further

ahead, that he would buy her a wheelchair soon after their case had been resolved and they had received their compensation.

From behind the Foremans, who were leaning against each other, the sun emerged, encircled in the twilight by a halo, its faint, cold light reflecting the pitiful image of man's bitter struggle and exposing the nature of his fragile body.

5

'The question might not have crossed your mind, ladies and gentlemen, but we do give it our utmost care and attention as part of our implicit responsibility to shoulder our next parliamentarian duty, to put things in their proper places for the sake of England's prosperity and for the stability of its economy and, primarily, the betterment of your personal wellbeing, whose burden we will carry; and should the oxygen run out we would make sure, if you had given us your votes, to provide it, bottled, to your doors. And you would not have to worry about the prices as, once we assume the seat of responsibility, we will then be compelled to put your "highly regarded" welfare before the welfare of the country, and vice versa...'

'Great! Lovely! Amazing!' rose the raucous sound of applause, from the palms of powerful hands.

Cheers of 'Long live the nominee!' were yelled out by mighty mouths, experienced at creating much fanfare.

Mr. Liam Hudson was addressing a small gathering of paid attendees, in a building on Sticky Trap Street, numbering twenty to twenty two of paid attendees, who one would expect to applaud even if they were in bed. The building was hastily drafted as a polling station, its facade decorated with electoral banners, and small and big posters of the council chairman.

The council chairman had chosen a sunny day, warm enough in view of the early cold onslaught, to deliver his speech. The snow had melted on most of the streets in the town. The unemployed came out in force to exercise or to shop.

At the beginning, Mr Hudson had resolved to remove Three Hills from his electoral campaign, adamant not to spend a single pound from the fund allocated for publicity. However, Mr Gallow persuaded him not to exclude Three Hills, even if his visit yielded only one vote. At the last moment, the council chairman gave in. He relented, after long, stubborn resistance, and went to Three Hills to give a speech, after he had delivered in four other cities four eloquent and stylistically modern speeches, the like of which England had never heard before.

But the sole vote coveted and dreamed of by both Mr Gallow and the council chairman had failed to turn up at the hall. The residents continued to pass by the building, tossing a black rose at its door as a sign of grief and as an act of condemnation following the death of Mr Foreman, who had passed away en route to the council building, as a result of a serious, cold-induced cramp of his tracheae.

While the nominee continued with his speech making, surrounded by his companions and disciples, applauded by the vociferous riffraff, whose shouting spilled over into the road, the polling vans roamed the town, carrying big posters and slogans, calling for people not to miss the opportunity to choose the nominee Liam Hudson, the most committed defender of people's rights, and sympathetic listener to their concerns.

The cars filled up the streets of Three Hills with screams and shouts blaring from loudspeakers, sowing annoyance right from Sticky Trap Street to the final houses on top of the three hills, where cows and sheep grazed the fields.

David felt he was retracting a memory whence thoughts sank, then floated, wet and dispersed, focusing on nothing in particular. He felt that his placidity was broken by the blaring and roaring of cars and that the loud speakers had intermingled with his thoughts, obliterating every trace from his memory.

The more eloquent the council chairman's speech, broadcast through the local FM radio station, became, the more enthusiastic became the passengers in the mobile polling van, and the louder their shrieks. This was coupled with the loud hooting of car horns that shook the glass of the windows, and caused the walls of houses to shrink, as if the situation were an embodiment of horror.

David had had enough of the uproar. He imagined that the cars were deliberately passing by his house to annoy him. He was not exactly sure why they were doing so! Or which sports team they were supporting! What was it all to do with him? Did he have to listen to these ear-shattering sounds to understand what they want?!

He felt that his head was cracking, about to explode because of the clamour targeting him. He frowned, mumbling words under his breath, his fury reaching a crescendo. All of a sudden he realised that his hearing was unblocked, cleared, allowing sounds to enter deep inside his ears and settle there. But instead of taking an interest in the return of his hearing, he rose to his feet, anger having got the better of him, opened the door and shouted at the top of his voice, 'Damn you all! Stop this pandemonium, you idiots!'

He slammed the door and returned to where he had been sitting. He felt that he had vented his rage. However, while he was sitting, he realised that posters of the council chairman and his name, written in big letters, were hoisted on the roofs of the cars. The raucous, squalling processions were but an electoral publicity procession.

He muttered to himself that the poster was the

council chairman's, Liam Hudson. He visualised the fleet of cars, and those men sticking the upper half of their bodies out the window. They were chanting and screaming Liam Hudson's name. Had he been nominated as an MP, I wonder?

His memory started to retrieve what he had seen on the street, then shifted to the council building and, afterwards to the officials' offices. Then it flitted toward his computer and office. He remembered the paperwork stacked up before him, the drawers with the files kept secure inside, and the shape of the office boy shoving at him the new data printouts, then leaving.

He rose to his feet and supported his temple against his hand as if feeling his brain cells open up one by one, only to be overwhelmed by the events and images, uninterrupted, intricate in their details, like a waterfall with its gushing water cascading, waves bumping against one another in their hurried descent into the abyss.

He expressed his astonishment at the revival of his awareness after a long absence, and the flight of things from his memory. He entered the kitchen as though seeking someone to tell, to explain to them the feelings and sensations he was experiencing, which nearly rendered him insane. Later, he went to the bedroom, talking animatedly with his hands about the return of the past, alive in front of him, in all its detail.

Then he ran back to the living room, hardly believing that his memory was responding to him, and that he was in full control of his sense of recall. He was able to retrieve any section or point, any dialogue, be it relevant to the recent past or to the earlier days.

There was nobody to share his exhilaration, and he had not yet come across anyone who stared at him in wide-eyed amazement at the event. He picked up the phone to call Fiona.

She asked, 'What happened?'

'Fiona, come back home, quickly!'

'Whatever happened to David?' she asked herself, going rapidly back home.

When David and his wife woke up together in the morning he shaved, then washed his face as usual, as though he was going to work; yet he stayed in the sitting room. When Fiona left, she bid him goodbye. He responded likewise. She closed the door after her. Sometimes, he did not hear what she was saying. At times he caught the last few sentences of the dialogue between them, often getting entangled and lost in the detail. Sometimes, the details became so mixed up that they began to wander away in his head, floating, struggling to achieve completion. This continued until Fiona came back from her hair-dressing salon.

So, what had prompted him today to contact her, urging her to come back home?!

'Has anything wrong happened to him? Has the

council come back to re-question him? However, he demands that I return home and has not mentioned the council!'

She imagined hundreds of scenarios while she hurried, stumbling across the pot holes and puddles of water. She made guesses about the minor or serious events that might have happened in her absence to David or to the house. She felt guilty about leaving him for long hours by himself, in his state of amnesia, self-neglect and the diseased condition that lasted a full year with no hope of recovery in sight.

She breathed in and held her breath, then said to herself, 'What if he discovered the money buried on top of the cupboard, rolled up in one of his socks. It would never cross anybody's mind that it was hidden among the old clothes!'

She was thinking very fast. She could see with her mind's eye the money falling into David's hands, and herself choosing a convenient explanation that would convince her husband that she did not hide it from him. Rather, she was doing it for their own benefit, or until he was cured of his indisposition! That she had received the cheque from the council and cashed it without his knowledge so that they might keep it for their future financial security.

She looked at the issue from every angle and wondered which explanation he would find credible. Would anyone be entitled to share that money with her, when she had kept it away from prying eyes? The issued cheque was in David's name as well as hers. That by no means meant it was David's, who was unconscious, unable to recall what was going on around him. He did not know why the cheque was issued in the first place; therefore, it was hers!

'But, perhaps...!' she said to herself, then she smiled a soft, knowing smile which soon grew wider, covering the rest of her countenance, 'He has touched himself and had an erection!'

She hurried up, consumed by the recent thought, preparing herself for the ensuing sweet expectations. She had been deprived of sex for a year. It was hard at the beginning, but she got used to it in the end; rather, she washed her hands of him and was no longer pressingly pursuing it.

But she recoiled within herself and now looked petrified with fear, quickening her pace, mumbling to herself, 'What if he has left the gas on and the kitchen has gone up in smoke, the house in ruins!'

With a nervous hand, anticipating the worse, she lowered the latch, pushing the hinge with force and calling out loudly, 'David!'

David came out of the kitchen when he heard her voice. He opened his arms wide and said, 'Fiona!' and held her in an embrace. 'My memory is back and my awareness is fully restored!'

Her fear vanished, her eyes overwhelmed by a

sparkle of surprise. 'Really!'

'Yes' he told her emphatically.

She then added, hugging him and pulling him towards her 'That's Fantastic!' then stood back while she was still looking at his face. 'When did this happen?'

'Half an hour ago. That's why I rang you so you would come.' He moved his arms up and down, overwhelmed with excitement. 'I wanted you to see it for yourself!'

Outside, the tooting and the hooting of vehicles drew closer for a moment, then faded away. Fiona took off her woollen overcoat and explained apologetically that she did not have much time, because she had left behind only one assistant. The happiness was gradually wiped from her face as she began pondering over the secret behind David's return of awareness. Therefore, she asked, 'Tell me, how did it happen? How do you know that... your memory has returned?'

'I can hardly believe it! I was sitting here feeling dejected by the boisterous activity of the polling campaign vehicles on the road outside. When I opened the door and saw the council manager's poster... the thoughts surged forward in my head. Then, I was stunned. I was able to hear very clearly. I went back to where I had been, and began to recall past events and, suddenly- I was overwhelmed by the uninterrupted flow of memories!'

Fiona listened intently to his account, observing his newly found cognitive ability and joy, though she, herself, was sceptical about what she was witnessing. She was desperate to grab something concrete with her mind, as it were or her hand, as to her, the cognitive ability of the observed was irrelevant. It was neither a testament to his ability to remember nor was it a proof of his recovered awareness.

'I couldn't believe what had happened to me,' David went on to say, noticing the perplexity on his wife's face. 'I was able to go back into the past, any point in the past, and still remember it in detail. Moreover, I can remember the very day we met at the club, when we went to Scarborough, and you were in your blue swimsuit. We laid down on the sand and ate ice-cream five successive times!' He kept smiling cheerfully. 'And our discussion of marriage! On that day your mum asked why I had to come on a bicycle to ask for your hand in marriage.' He held Fiona by the arms. 'Don't you remember?'

'What else?' Fear and suspicion intermingled on her face.

'You obviously do not believe me!' he said, taken aback by her nonchalance.

Having exhausted all her patience, she finally asked, 'David! Why are you here? I mean, at home!'

Putting his face in his hands, astonished she should ask such a question, he replied: 'Because the council has not yet resolved my issue. They accuse me of squandering public money!'

'How? I mean, in what way?'

'I sent a cheque to every household in Three Hills,' he said.

'Ah...' Fiona collapsed in the armchair, covering her head with her hands.

He looked at her in astonishment, failing to comprehend her confusion. His thoughts wandered away as he began to remember the interrogation at the council with the council chairman shouting and breathing down his neck, and the questioning by the technical and administrative committees, and the secrecy surrounding all that.

He now felt that the situation had changed. It was Fiona's turn who now had her thoughts wandered off, plunging her into the unconscious. She became withdrawn as she sat in a chair, while he stood confidently answering her questions.

Then he became impatient with the role-play. He detested the investigators and the yelling of the council chairman. But now he wanted to know the reason for his wife's confusion, when she was supposed to be pleased with his recovery from an indisposition that almost turned him into a corpse, cast aside at home.

Could it be that she was concerned about the consequences and the ramifications that would follow from mishandling public money? He was willing to confront the council, standing in front of them with his tall slender figure to say 'Yes', that he did indeed send out the money to all Three Hills' residents and that he was unrepentant!

A period of silence prevailed between them. He stood, disconcerted, while she sat, staring at the ceiling, contemplating a way out of this unexpected impasse which had taken her by surprise.

'David,' she asked calmly, straightening up her sitting position, 'did you squander the council's money?'

'Yes, I did!' he answered temperately, awaiting what lurked behind her question.

Fiona retained her position, pondered over the ragged stocking, wrapped around the money, tossed amongst the old clothes, afraid of an unexpected storm that she had failed to predict, failed to take into account throughout the recent months.

Should she tell him that she had received the cheque and cashed it without telling him? Should she hide it from him and act as though the money was not there? Or should she fetch the money and place it before him and say, 'You did the right thing when you squandered the council's money, and this is our free share of their coffer!'

However, David had not yet made any reference to the total value of the money he sent out to the residents. He did not disclose that he had allocated ten thousand pounds to this house, their house. Would it be easy to distract him and push the amount from his mind, or perhaps force him into explicitly admitting to it?

'Suppose,' she said finally, 'you acted the way you did. Did you ever think of the consequences? Had you ever considered your responsibility for such a reckless act?' Fiona readjusted her sitting posture, shifting her weight to the edge of the sofa.

'Suppose?! How do I suppose? And why do you call it a reckless act?' asked David, with signs of incredulity at what his wife had just said, appearing on his face. 'Yes, I did what was dictated by my conscience, come what may in the end!'

'Calm down, dear!' said Fiona, trying to placate him tenderly, while he was obviously answering her very calmly. 'We need to understand why you have done it! We need to know if you are aware of the limits and confines of your responsibilities when you sent out those cheques!'

'Of course I do!' David retorted defensively. 'And I do realise that Three Hills' residents actually deserved that amount,'

'Forget about Three Hills residents!' Fiona interrupted him in an attempt to distract him from talking about the residents and the sums of money. 'I am thinking about your responsibility as an official, about your integrity and your reputation among the people!'

David detected a measure of loyalty, some interest in his good name and reputation at the council. He walked up and down the living room, contemplating what she said. But, no sooner had he stood in front of her that his good name and reputation retreated from his head to say in a low voice, 'You cannot understand the council accounts. Neither can you imagine the amounts surreptitiously plucked away from the people! All is based on fraud, on theft. Millions go into their coffers. Then it quickly disappears. No one knows how those millions, those huge sums, have been spent! Nobody knows the mysterious people in whose names this money go. But I do!'

While he was talking, Fiona kept looking at him, thinking of what to say, and in which direction she wanted to steer him.

'Responsibility! There's no such thing as responsibility in that rotten building!' he continued, maintaining the full vent he has given to his feelings. 'There is no compassion. Corruption alone is having a ball there! Trust me!'

An idea crossed her mind, lingering in her head for a while, pushing back all thoughts. Encouraged by the prevalent calm on the street, she rose to her feet to face him, overcoming her initial fear. She took him in her arms, pulling him closer. 'David, you talk like a dreamer. I am concerned for your health and well-being,'

'How?' he asked while he was in her arms. 'I do not dream!'

'Oh, yes, you do, you are exhausted, my love,' she retorted calmly, still holding him tightly but tenderly.

'But you don't believe in me,' he muttered, still in her arms, feeling let down.

'About what?' she asked.

'About my being able to confront them.'

'Forget about it!'

She leaned her head against his chest, while David wondered inwardly what she might be ambiguously referring to. Affection was reciprocal as he placed his hands on her shoulders for a while, feeling the comfort of hugging her. At the same time he explored the corridors of his memory in search of what prompted her to say those words. Did she not want him to talk about the issue now? Or drop the subject altogether and forget about it, for fear of losing his job and suffering the ramifications that would follow?

He had a peaceable nature and, like her, could not stand offending a human being. He had never entertained the idea. However, being aware of fraud and corruption occurring before his very eyes made his blood boil, and silence was no longer an option.

Apart from this, sending a command to the computer to print out cheques was a manifestation of discontent, signalling the beginning of an outburst of anger which had accumulated deep inside him. It was only the diseased condition which had scattered his attention and prevented him from blowing the whistle sooner, uncovering the secrets and laying the truths out before the people!

'Perhaps retreat is out of the question now,' he mumbled to himself. He released her, and the cuddle slowly disentangled.

Should he confess to paying out the cheques, they would hold him accountable. He would lose his job and be thrown into jail, and the whole story would be forgotten, with no opportunity to raise the issue he had long set out to raise and provoke!

Once again he paced up and down the living room, while Fiona watched him, nervous, sceptical about his intentions, trying to fathom out what he was scheming. She said, taking off her coat and slinging it on the sofa, 'I am boiling some water for a quick cup of coffee. Would you like to join me?'

'No, thank you,' he replied. His thoughts were scattered all over the place. Then he added, standing in her way, 'Listen, I cannot possibly go back now. All will be lost.'

'Oh, David, my love, haven't we gone through that?' She went closer to him, taking his hand in hers.

'Gone through what?' he asked in puzzlement. 'I haven't even started and I want you to support me!'

‘Support you with what?’ It was her turn to ask now, pretending she did not understand the issue he was discussing. She left him moving confusedly through clouds of his own making, while she sailed away.

‘If I don’t expose their methods, they’ll devour me like a dollop of butter on a fraction of biscuit. I’ve got myself involved, and I have to carry it through till the end, otherwise I offer my neck into their claws!’

Fiona commented, laughing, mocking his exaggerations, ‘“Got myself involved”! Now, you are talking like a cartoon hero!’ Her comment showered cold water over his words.

‘I know they falsify documents that show imaginary taxes. I know about the transactions they strike with the companies, which involve millions of pounds. And I also know the licenses granted to charities which allow them to collect funds in their name. I am privy to the secrets of all their accounts!’

‘Don’t forget that these are the secrets they have entrusted you with, haven’t they?’ she said, giving him a word of warning.

‘But they are a pack of lies, and the law makes them answerable for these acts! People continue to pay up, unaware of any malpractice!’

‘Why worry about other people. They are not our concern!’

‘I can’t believe you are saying these words!’ he said in astonishment.

'Believe what?' She stared at him with astonishment.

'What you just said!'

'Of course, because you are talking about delusions!'

'Delusions?' he asked in disbelief.

'Yes, delusions. You sometimes dream of this; at times of that. Actually you dream aloud. This condition of yours is recurring. You, ever the accuser of officials in government, the system and all people around you. You will not rest until your fury is well and truly vented, only to relapse, then, into your stupor of absent-mindedness.' She picked up her coat from the settee. 'I am running late for the salon. I need to get back.'

'Wait! I do not hallucinate, if that is what you are insinuating!' protested David. She took her time in leaving, while he went on to say, 'Moreover, I don't dream things up! I know a great deal, and if I don't expose them, they will walk over me and I will be lost in the stampede!'

Seeking to undermine him, she said apathetically, and slightly patronizingly, 'You don't know anything!'

'Oh! Yes, I do!'

'No, this is megalomania! You've been afflicted with it every two or three months now, then you will be crushed anew by your indisposition.' She finished her observation while simultaneously looking at her wrist watch. She continued to sow the seeds of self-doubt and undermine his self-confidence as she added, 'Even while you're asleep, you're visited by these dreams, and quite often I hear you utter weird things!'

'You don't mean that, do you?'

'Of course I do!' she responded emphatically. 'And when these fits and hallucinations are over, you thrust your thumb into your mouth and sleep like a baby!'

From the corner of his eye, he looked at his thumb then smiled. 'You must be joking…'

'Not at all!' came the firm response, turning her face toward the other side.

They moved away from each other, trying to collect their thoughts independently. While Fiona looked pensive, with her hand on the edge of the sofa, she was, nevertheless, distraught, as it were; waiting for what might come out of his head, ready to respond with a counterattack. David imagined himself as a toddler, fast asleep, foetus-like, in bed, sucking his thumb. Once again, a smile appeared on his face and he made his final pronouncement. 'If you must insist on these delusions, then what about the cheque you received like the others?'

'What?' she asked him, aghast.

'The cheque which arrived last November.' He looked her in the eye now. 'Was *that* a "delusion"?'

'What cheque? You must be in your dotage!' she retorted obstinately.

'Am I correct in saying that you have already cashed

it?' he asked in a composed tone.

'I don't know what cheque you are talking about!' she responded emphatically.

'In November I authorised the payment of ten thousand pound to every household, to mark the beginning of my rebellion! Or would you put that down to "delusions" as well?' he stressed.

'Unprecedented nonsense!' she responded with confidence, adding, 'Your fertile imagination is beginning to give out thousands to Three Hills households.' She let out a sardonic guffaw, pitching her voice as though she was addressing a crowd. 'O people of Three Hills! King Solomon is placing thousands of pounds on your doorstep!' She burst into a hysterical and mocking laugh, then went into the bedroom, her laughter trailing behind.

David stood still, aghast, listening to the laughter coming from the bedroom. He couldn't comprehend the significance of her conduct or understand her intentions. When the laughter stopped, Fiona appeared, carrying a small box. She poured its contents onto the low table and said softly, 'This is all we have in our possession: seven hundred and twenty pounds. I managed to save it out of your salary and mine. We need to pay out of it the council tax, the rent and every other utility bill and credit card we have. Here! Please, count it.'

After a moment's silence, shifting his gaze from the

money to her face, he asked, 'And the ten thousand pounds?'

'The ten thousand pounds! Go to the neighbours and ask them to see if they indeed received such an amount. Besides, tell them about your madness, your delusions, in staging a rebellion for their benefit. Tell them that you will lead a revolution that will burn the world down until the council is held accountable and the people feel justice is done.' Defiant, she looked him in the eye, her arms akimbo, awaiting his response.

'That's impossible! I don't believe this!' He stood dumbfounded, in bewilderment, struggling to come to terms with a choice between believing her claims and trusting his own judgement based on his awareness of the obvious.

She sat down, somewhat exhausted, after detecting the early signs of self-doubt and shaken confidence.

He began talking to himself. 'There seems to be some grey area lying between one's memory and the facts offered to him.' Then he carried on in louder voice, albeit calmly, 'I know what my memory is telling me, though I don't see why you should find that doubtful. I am quite certain that the cheques were sent out to the households of Three Hills, including ours, this house. But, you still deny it, as if you are deliberately fogging my brain, veiling my eyes. What are trying to achieve by that? Where do you want me to end up?'

She pleaded with him to listen. 'I do not put a veil over your eyes. I certainly do not seek to mislead you, believe me. I'm only trying to make you see sense. Talking about the cheque... The ten thousands are nothing but a figment of your imagination! There was no cheque, David, and that is the truth! If you wish we had a big sum of money then, that is very well intentioned, whether it is for us or for the residents of Three Hills. But, mind you, intentions do no go beyond what they are. Do you understand me?'

'Intentions?' He held on tightly to his awareness, though with shadows of doubt rising and falling within.

'We all dream of doing the best for others,' she continued in a soft, submissive tone, attempting to fragment his convictions. 'We can't possibly demand that they return the dream to us, or hold them to account, can we?'

David as though, he was having a soliloquy. 'Even if the people of Three Hills deny it, I still have a feeling, floating around my senses, telling me that I have set it in motion, whether the cheque has arrived or has been stolen by the rag-tag angels!'

She let out a loud guffaw, then, gesturing at him she said, 'Look at this sick man who is being paid by the government. Yet, he is determined to deliver it a blow to prove, and only to prove, that he is no less deserving of the salary than the other officials!'

He talked as though he was away from her, with confidence that was gradually gaining momentum, 'I have carried out what I had been thinking about for two years or more and... Tomorrow when I go back to them I will confront them face-to-face. I will tell them every thing I know from A to Z!'

'And risk losing everything, mark my words!' she warned, to frustrate him.

He was still away from her, talking quietly but with determination. 'Afterwards I will hold a news conference to expose their tricks. I will let my voice reach Downing Street! That's my plan.'

'They will laugh at your imbecility in Downing Street. They will make fun of your naivety, and after five minutes they will fold it away! They can't find the time to determine its credibility.' She is making comments, pretending not to take him seriously enough but she still fearful. She tried to interrupt his train of thought, then quickly snatched her coat from the sofa and put it on, pretending she was going out.

She said, emotionally blackmailing him, 'There's no point listening to this nonsense and there's no use giving you advice! Stay where you are, in your chimera.' Again acting as though she was getting ready to go, she fumbled in her pockets to delay herself.

He continued, unaware of her antics. 'Thanks to the council chairman, special thanks to the huge posters mounted on car tops and the riffraff who have been crowing out his name, for bringing back my memory! And bringing me back to my senses, to the abominable reality we live in.'

She picked on his reference to the posters and the crowing, ready to bounce into action. She had a new plan to entrap him. She said: 'What posters are you babbling about?'

'Liam Hudson's,' he replied as though he was suddenly aware for the first time, of her presence, 'I had to be grateful for their clamour and the crowing of their cars, which blasted my senses into action and woke me up from the oppressive absence of my mind!'

'Listen to the product of visualisation!' she is quick to say, Just wait for what fantasy my husband has created while he is awake!'

She went towards the door and opened it, but had second thoughts and returned to the chair. 'There, go and look for yourself and listen. See if there is crowing on the street, posters and cars' clamour! Go and have a look so that we may end the subject!'

'What do you mean?' he asked, his sight tentatively focused on the void between Fiona and the open door.

'The clamour! It is clamour of your own makingwhich you are referring to!' She responded while she was sitting, pretending to be relieved. 'Take a look! See if there are cars hooting and tooting on the street. Let's put an end to your delusions!'

David rose to his feet uncertainly, aware of the peace and quiet prevailing on the street, but equally oblivious to whether Fiona, judging by her nonchalant sitting posture, was indeed certain about what she was saying.

'Go!' she raised her outstretched arm towards the door. 'See for yourself if there are cars.'

Tentatively, and slowly, David made for the door. He stopped, looked right then left. He suddenly turned around to face Fiona, disbelief written all over his face. He cast another look. He closed the door and went back to where he was, his self-confidence badly shaken. A period of profound silence and perplexity descended upon them.

'But I did see everything!' he said defensively at last. 'The cars and the crowing of men! The loud noise was all there! Resonating and shaking the house in the process!'

Feeling his forehead, he searched inside his head for evidence he could produce, while Fiona, looking relaxed, sat on the sofa, happy with the outcome, eyeing him from the corner of her eye, uncertainly and with suspicion.

'Out of the question!' He circled her in disbelief, scouring his memory for a proof to back up what he was saying all along. Finally he said, 'The noise was so loud, it gave me a headache. Moreover, I had to yell at them!'

The deeper his bewilderment, the more his self-confidence deteriorated.

When Fiona was convinced his self-confidence was shaken, she got up and took off her coat again and threw it on the sofa. She moved closer to him and appealed to his reason. 'You witnessed the quietness on the street. What more do you want?' She took his hand tenderly and spoke to him appealingly. 'Discard these illusions. Push them to the back of your head. Get rid of them, my love. Thinking too long about them will only prompt you to invent more and will ultimately drown you. Come over here, darling. Take a deep breath so as to drive these strange thoughts out of your mind…'

He was in two minds, caught between believing what she said, and trusting what he felt with his own senses. Memories, visualisations and plans, all pushing one another ahead, toward the front of the brain, where they seemed to disperse. He said, 'But, the reality is quite the opposite!' He wrenched one of his hands free from hers, saying 'My inner self confirms other issues to me.'

She interrupted him with a warning, 'do not put your faith in reality, but push it out from your mind. Try to imagine there is nothing as important as your health. You have suffered a lot. You have had to put up with so much, and I will have to put up with yet more to ensure your full recovery.' David freed his other hand while she went on in the same unbridled tone. 'You have gone a long way en route to recovery, from this indisposition; I have monitored the improvement you have achieved with joy. So why on earth do you chase after trivialities? Things that do not concern you, and their invention can only drain you?'

David was retreating, while Fiona stepped towards him, pressing ahead with her advice in an attempt to blind him and deaden his heart and move him away from consciousness.

'I don't invent them,' he retorted, calmly but emphatically. 'They come from here!' He pointed to himself 'I have been thinking about them in my periods of absent-mindedness. I used to consider them in my halved awareness. They'd often slip away, then re-emerge in my consciousness. These are not the product of a demented imagination. Why don't you consider it in depth?'

She finally gave up, but she was still optimistic. Fiona resumed her former sitting position, depressed. She spoke in an audible voice as if she were talking to herself, moving her hands forward in an animated way as though she was communicating with an invisible person.

'There is no point! I want to save him from the chaos of his delusions and the paradox of his words, yet he resolutely reverts to it! Fiona, this is yet another manifestation that he is losing it!'

'That is not the case!' he asserted with confidence, but signs of early fatigue were showing through.

'You need to let him swim, chasing dreams till he drops!' She continued her soliloquy. 'Fiona! You've done your bit, as best as you can as a loyal wife; you have pointed out to him the evidence and the indications but they obviously have all fallen on deaf ears. What more could you have done?'

After a period of silence he suddenly protested, 'Why do you doubt my awareness?'

'Me? I don't, but I have grown tired of running after you, with you chasing shadows in the dark.'

'As my wife, you are supposed to stand by me!' he said, as though looking for an answer within himself.

'You, yourself refuse to let me stand by your side!' she retorted, procrastinating and continued as if she were taking to herself, 'How can I keep up with you when your imagination conjures up images of cars hooting and flying in space? Where do you want me to stand, while you are giving out cheques without any restraint to the residents of Three Hills? Why should I obey you while you are deeply engrossed in quixotic fights, brandishing your sabre in the face of the councils, governments and their businesses, to bring them down, leaving them behind, stumbling confusedly in a trail of blood? I have never heard you saying a reasonable thing that was accepted by my small brain and yet, deliberately ignored my advice!'

David pondered over what she was saying. He felt sorry for both of them, because the schism was widening and he was unable bridge it up. Besides, retracting his ideas was not possible. He sat on the chair opposite at a loss, thinking over and over again of the hooting of the vehicles. He could think of no justification for the disappearance of these vehicles and the uproar they had created.

Indeed, he yelled at them, and the cry was still ringing in his ears. But what did he want them to do when he shouted? What did he say? he wondered. He wanted to remember the words he had uttered, but they had vanished from his head! Damn! Did he yell at them to keep them off the house! Or what?

Then he moved on to the council. His thoughts escaped to its building. He stood before its chairman, Liam Hudson, surrounded by the officials resembling a flock of sheep, waiting for the charges to be called out. They watched his mouth, waiting expectantly for him to utter the damning evidence, to reveal what information he had gathered and what he knew about the corruption, the secrets of fraud and deception. But the words failed him.

All the words that had begun to circulate in his mind half an hour ago, the cases he had prepared and the chronological order in which they would be announced, and the facts he had established, all had gone in a puff of smoke. He could hardly remember a word. They left no trace in his memory.

'How did all that happen? What's happening to my memory?' he murmured. Words quivered on his lips. Meanwhile, Fiona kept her eyes on the floor, surreptitiously looking at him, catching what slipped off his tongue.

He felt that his memory had gone. Thoughts which moments ago flowed out to overwhelm him had now abandoned him. His awareness was crushed, destroyed. Information and revolutions retreated into the dark corridors of a ruined unconscious. He was incapable of focusing on a single thing in particular.

Fiona stood up to take off her coat and throw it again on the sofa. She held out her hand, inviting him, 'Come over here. What did I tell you?'

'Yes, I was talking about the council, wasn't I?' he responded absent-mindedly, but it was a rhetorical question.

'Come, don't let yourself be weighed down with worries.' She still offered her hand to him, and he finally responded, lifting his hand into the void for Fiona to hold. She helped him stand up.

'But what does the council want from me?' he asked inattentively.

Fiona took him by the hand and sat him next to her on the sofa, covering parts of his body and hugging him.

'The council...' he said repeatedly, yielding in her

arms like a little lamb.

'Stop worrying, because thinking aggravates your indisposition.' She rocked him in her lap as she would a baby to make him go to sleep.

The telephone rang and she ignored it. David was asleep in her lap, his thumb in his mouth. He sucked it like a baby.

'Do you remember our summer trip to the sea? We were in Whitby, not Scarborough, and I was wearing a red swimsuit, adorned with golden threads across the chest, not a blue one... We were sitting on the sand eating fish 'n' chips, not ice-cream. My mum was with us and we were not on our own. She was pouring hot tea from a thermos...'

The telephone rang again and continued to ring. She paid it no attention.

Printed in EU by Pulsio SARL